Exploring Inner Space

PERSONAL EXPERIENCES UNDER LSD-25

by Jane Dunlap

Exploring Inner Space

Personal Experiences Under LSD-25

by Jane Dunlap

pseudonym for Adelle Davis

ISHI PRESS INTERNATIONAL

Exploring Inner Space
Personal Experiences Under LSD-25

by Jane Dunlap

First Published in 1961

This Printing in June, 2013
by Ishi Press in New York and Tokyo
with a new introduction by Sam Sloan

ISBN 4-87187-960-7
978-4-87187-960-6

Ishi Press International
1664 Davidson Avenue, Suite 1B
Bronx NY 10453-7877
USA
1-917-507-7226

Printed in the United States of America

Introduction by Sam Sloan

Exploring Inner Space

Personal Experiences Under LSD-25

by Jane Dunlap

Pseudonym for Adelle Davis

Introduction by Sam Sloan

Jane Dunlap's book is an account of a series of experiments, conducted through the medium of LSD-25, then a recently discovered and extremely powerful hallucinogenic drug. The author of this book volunteered to be the subject of an early experiment employing lysergic acid diethylamide, or LSD-25. Her duty was to record in detail her visions while under the drug. She used the pseudonym Jane Dunlap for reasons that became obvious when her true identity was revealed.

LSD-25 is simply the long form of the drug LSD. There is no difference between LSD and LSD-25.

LSD has been used with apparent success by many famous people. Steve Jobs, CEO of Apple Inc., said, "Taking LSD was a profound experience, one of the most important things in my life."

LSD was tremendously popular in the 1960s and this book may have contributed to the popularity. LSD did not became illegal in California until October 6, 1966. It was not made illegal under federal law until 1970. By the 1970s, it came to be regarded as a dangerous drug even by those who had advocated its use in the 1960s. As a result, it became no longer fashionable to "Drop Acid".

In retrospect, it seems strange that a fitness guru and nutritionist Adelle Davis would write in a book that she had taken LSD. However, there may be a connection. Organic foods became fashionable in the Early 1960s, at about the same time that LSD became fashionable. It is likely that members of the hippie generation that were eating organic foods were also dropping acid.

Nowadays, the Adelle Davis Foundation is a 501(c)3 not for profit. It proudly lists this book, **Personal Experiences Under LSD-25**, as one of the books by Adelle Davis.

Adelle Davis is an incredibly famous and popular author whose name and whose books have reached the household word status. Her recommendations are followed by millions today. She is the leading spokesperson for the organic foods movement. She is known for popularizing the phrase "You Are What You Eat". When you see organic food stores all over and special organic foods shelves in supermarkets, think of Adelle Davis as the person who popularized all of this.

However, she digressed from her usual persona to write this book, **Personal Experiences Under LSD-25** under the pseudonym of **Jane Dunlap.**

She was born in Lizton, Indiana on February 25,

1904. Her first book was Optimum Health published in 1935. This book did not have a publisher. The first book to make her famous was a cook book published in 1947: ***Let's Cook it Right***. This was followed by **Let's Have Healthy Children** (1951) and **Let's Eat Right to Keep Fit** (1954).

Her movement became popular because of the increased use of pesticides, chemicals, additives and fertilizers to increase food production.

Davis wrote a series of four books, starting with a cookbook in 1947, that ultimately sold over 10 million copies in total. Although her ideas were considered somewhat eccentric in the 1940s and 1950s, the change in culture with the 1960s brought her ideas, especially her anti-food processing and food industry charges, into the mainstream in a time when anti-authority sentiment was growing. She also contributed to, as well as benefited from, the rise of a nutritional and health food movement that began in the 1950s, which focused on subjects such as pesticide residues and food additives, a movement her critics would come to term food faddism. During the 1960s and 1970s, her popularity continued to grow, as she was featured in multiple media reports, variously described as an "oracle" by the New York Times, "high priestess" by Life and was compared to Ralph Nader, the popular consumer activist, by the Associated Press. Her celebrity was demonstrated by her repeated guest appearances on The Tonight Show Starring Johnny Carson, as she became the most popular and influential nutritionist in the country.

Let us say that her works have not been without criticism. Critics state that there is no scientific proof for some of her claims, especially her claims that non-organic foods are a significant health risk. She is also criticized recommending for large doses of Vitamin A and Vitamin D. However, her nutritional ideas such as the need for exercise, the dangers of vitamin deficiencies as well as the need to avoid hydrogenated fat, saturated fat and excess sugar consumption remain relevant to even mainstream nutritionists.

Her followers were shocked when Adelle Davis developed cancer at age 70. She was shocked too as she had contended that almost any disease could be prevented by proper diet. When she contracted the cancer that later killed her, she maintained that it did not invalidate her theories about proper diet. She attributed the illness to the junk food she had eaten at college. She wrote:

> "I think that I am sympathetic with the people who are quite annoyed with the fact that I have cancer. When I was told I had it I could not believe it either. I thought this was for people who drink soft drinks, who eat white bread, who eat refined sugar and so on."

However, then she realized that her diet had changed when she went to Purdue University at age 19. From 1924 to the early 1950 she ate

“Commercial Junk Food”. She blamed this plus her heavy work load and a series of Xray examinations on the fact that he had cancer. Note that she did not list taking LSD as a possible cause of her problems.

Adelle Davis died on 31 May 1974 in Los Angeles, having gone there to die knowing that her life was at its end.

Adelle Davis' fitness books are simple. sound and above all practical guides to the principles of nutrition. “Nutrition is a personal matter," says Miss Davis, "as personal as your diary or income tax report. Your nutrition can determine, how you look, act, and feel; whether you are grouchy or cheerful, homely or beautiful, whether you think clearly or are confused, enjoy your work or make it a drudgery.”

Let's Eat Right To Keep Fit is designed to help any normal adult find his or her way to maximum fitness through proper diet. The book discusses the sixty or more nutrients needed by the body to build health, and tells what foods supply these nutrients in the most concentrated form. The essential vitamins and minerals are dealt with in detail, and their function in the body analyzed according to the most up-to-date medical information. Miss Davis then makes specific recommendations for a balanced diet supplying- adequate quantities of all these vital substances. In a final section, the author discusses the general aspects of the nutrition problem, and tells what the individual can do to help build national health.

Introduction by Sam Sloan

Business executives throughout the country who are faced with problems of stress and anxiety will find this book an invaluable aid in keeping themselves and their employees in top health. And - like her other successes in the field of nutrition, Let's Cook It Right and Let's Have Healthy Children - Adelle Davis' book has been widely read and used in the home as a guide to better living.

ADELLE DAVIS was a consulting nutritionist in Los Angeles. She studied at Purdue University, Columbia, the University of California, and U.C.L.A., and had a Master of Science degree from the University of Southern California Medical School. She served as a dietitian at Bellevue Hospital in New York City, and as Supervisor of Health Education in the public schools of Yonkers, New York.

Sam Sloan
San Rafael, California
USA
June 16, 2013

Original Back and Side Flaps

JANE DUNLAP

Exploring Inner Space

PERSONAL EXPERIENCES UNDER LSD-25

Introduction by Robert S. Davidson, Ph.D., Clinical Psychologist

Although vision-producing substances, such as peyote cactus and certain types of mushrooms, have been used in religious ceremonies for hundreds, possibly thousands of years, a detailed account of the visions has never been published. Now, under rigid medical supervision, studies of the effects of hallucinogens are being carried out. The author of this book volunteered to be the subject of such an experiment, this one employing lysergic acid diethylamide, or LSD-25. Her duty was to record in detail her visions while under the drug.

Because these vividly clear accounts touch upon matters of deep spiritual meaning as well as clinical purport, it was decided to publish them. Because they are so intensely self-revealing, often intimate, the author-a nationally known writer-chose to use the pseudonym Jane Dunlap.

Exploring Inner Space is highly individual-unlike any book ever published. It is impossible to predict its effect upon the reader. Some may find in it merely an intriguing account of a mind roving dramatically free; others may react to its emotional range-from sheer terror to utter bliss; still others may find here the spiritual response they have never been able to articulate for themselves. The properties and possible uses of LSD are discussed by Dr. Robert S. Davidson in his introduction and in an appendix.

Jacket design by Arthur Hawkins

"LSD is one of the most recent and the most powerful in a series of hallucinogenic drugs. The term hallucinogenic refers to the peculiar property of these drugs, when taken into a person's body, of inducing a mental state in which appear fantastic visions, often in the most brilliant colors. Together with the visions, the subject taking one of these drugs may experience perceptual distortions of his surroundings and of his body itself, perhaps along with anxiety, intense emotions of all kinds, excitement, and, at times, fragmentation of thought. One cannot predict in advance what the hallucinogenic experience will be. The visions may be awe inspiring in their grandeur and beauty or monstrous in their horrible nightmare quality. Almost always the subject is introduced to such increased awareness that this experience remains one of the outstanding events of his life. Certain fortunate subjects, perhaps one fourth of those who take the drug, have profound mystical experiences."
-From the introduction

Original Back and Side Flaps

From the Introduction by Dr. Davidson:

My host concluded the introductions at his party, "And this is Jane Dunlap."

I looked down into a pair of laughing blue eyes and immediately felt I had found a friend. We had started the usual small talk when my attention suddenly was caught by the name tag thoughtfully provided by our host to help faulty memories.

"You're not the Jane Dunlap!" I cried, thinking of how eagerly we had looked forward to each of her books.

Of course, she was Jane Dunlap, a household word now become a lively, husky-voiced reality, a woman sparkling with vitality and good humor, refreshingly direct and sincere in her manner. This Jane Dunlap was a woman of fearless opinions, well read, intelligent, and above all a warm human being.

As we talked on, the conversation somehow turned to a discussion of lysergic acid diethylamide, or LSD-25, a powerful hallucinogenic, or vision-producing, drug under study as an aid to psychotherapy. Miss Dunlap excitedly asked about my experience with it from my standpoint both as a person who had taken it some twenty-five times and as a psychologist working with volunteer research subjects. She had had one unforgettable experience with it through a local university and had already volunteered to be a subject in the research being carried on by my colleague, Dr. Oscar Janiger, a psychiatrist who is studying its effects on the release of creative potential in artists, writers and musicians. From this chance meeting developed our subsequent collaboration in the LSD experiments she describes in this book.

From the British Edition

Our break-through into outer space has caught everyone's imagination, but posterity may well find that it is of less fundamental significance than the experiments which are being simultaneously conducted in the exploration of inner space-that is, of the universe within the mind.

Jane Dunlap's book is an account of one such series of experiments, conducted through the medium of LSD-25, a recently discovered and extremely powerful hallucinogenic drug.

SCIENTIFIC BOOK CLUB EDITION

Dedicated to those wonderful stagehands who helped pull back the curtains

CONTENTS

INTRODUCTION: *A Psychologist Explains*

by Robert S. Davidson, Ph.D., Clinical Psychologist

MY HOST concluded the introductions at his party, "And this is Jane Dunlap."

I looked down into a pair of laughing blue eyes and immediately felt I had found a friend. We had started the usual small talk when my attention suddenly was caught by the name tag thoughtfully provided by our host to help faulty memories.

"You're not *the* Jane Dunlap!" I cried, thinking of how eagerly we had looked forward to each of her books.

Of course, she was Jane Dunlap, a household word now become a lively, husky-voiced reality, a woman sparkling with vitality and good humor, refreshingly direct and sincere in her manner. This Jane Dunlap was a woman of fearless opinions, well read, intelligent, and above all a warm human being.

As we talked on, the conversation somehow turned to a

Readers wishing to learn more of the scientific aspects of lysergic acid diethylamide are referred to the appendix, p. 210, also written by Dr. Davidson.

discussion of lysergic acid diethylamide, or LSD-25, a powerful hallucinogenic, or vision-producing, drug under study as an aid to psychotherapy. Miss Dunlap excitedly asked about my experience with it from my standpoint both as a person who had taken it some twenty-five times and as a psychologist working with volunteer research subjects. She had had one unforgettable experience with it through a local university and had already volunteered to be a subject in the research being carried on by my colleague, Dr. Oscar Janiger, a psychiatrist who is studying its effects on the release of creative potential in artists, writers, and musicians. From this chance meeting developed our subsequent collaboration in the LSD experiments she describes in this book.

Essentially, Miss Dunlap's book is a report. It is part of a research study. It would have been written, as indeed most of it was written, with no thought of publication. Miss Dunlap volunteered to be a subject in a scientific experiment. Her duty as a subject was to take, under proper psychiatric supervision, a clinically tested medication, lysergic acid diethylamide, and then to report back to the experimenters exactly what her response to this medication was.

As investigators, we are faced with the complex problem of trying to be scientifically objective about very subjective personal experiences. The only way we can hope to approach objectivity is to accumulate many records of the effects of the drug. Some drugs can be dropped onto cultures of bacteria growing in little glass dishes. We can see what happens to the bacteria; either they die or they continue to grow and thrive. LSD cannot be tested in such a simple way because its primary effect is on the brain and the mind of the subject. Though there are devices for recording some of the processes going on in the brains of test animals and human beings, the only way we have of knowing what goes on in the mind is for the subjects to tell us. Consequently, the subjects' reports are invaluable to the researcher. Miss Dunlap's accounts, together with the reports and standardized questionnaires of hundreds of other volunteers, are now being analyzed to determine how lysergic acid can best be used in releasing the potentials of the human mind.

LSD is one of the most recent and the most powerful in a series of hallucinogenic drugs. The term hallucinogenic refers to the peculiar property of these drugs, when taken into a person's body, of inducing a mental state in which appear fantastic visions, often in the most brilliant colors. Together with the visions, the subject taking one of these drugs may experience perceptual distortions of his surroundings and of his body itself, perhaps along with anxiety, intense emotions of all kinds, excitement, and, at times, fragmentation of thought. One cannot predict in advance what the hallucinogenic experience will be. The visions may be awe inspiring in their grandeur and beauty or monstrous in their horrible nightmare quality. Almost always the subject is introduced to such increased awareness that this experience remains one of the outstanding events of his life. Certain fortunate subjects, perhaps one fourth of those who take the drug, have profound mystical experiences.

The vision-producing drugs have a long history. As far back as knowledge of man exists, there have been stories of herbs, roots, brews, and potions to be eaten, drunk, or smoked to change in some way the state of consciousness. The mythical nepenthe, or dissolver of sorrows, of ancient Greece was supposed to bring forgetfulness. Thousands of years ago in India the juice of a plant called soma was used as a sacred drink in religious ceremonies. This juice was supposed to make those fortunate ones who were permitted to drink it feel happy and full of love and spiritual insight.

Soma eventually passed out of use, and today we know nothing quite like it.

As long ago as 1000 B.C., Eastern literature contained stories of the use of a drug now known and used all over the world under a variety of names including Indian hemp (hashish) and marihuana. Traditionally the uses of this plant, technically known as *Cannabis sativa,* have varied from a sacred one in religious ceremonies to a profane one in inciting assassins to kill.

Our own Western hemisphere has contributed several hallucinogens. Before the time of Columbus, the Indians in Mexico were using peyote in religious ceremonies. Peyote is the variety of cactus whose vision-producing ingredient is mescaline. This use continues on into the present time and into our own Southwestern states. The Aztecs in Mexico used sacred mushrooms in their religious ceremonies, and the traditions have been handed down to the present.

It has been said that the berserkers, a group of wild and fierce Norse warriors, acquired their reckless courage by eating a variety of hallucinogenic mushroom. Four other natural hallucinogenic agents, not so widely known, have also been used to some extent, primarily by primitive tribes in Latin America. Some synthetic, or man-made, drugs also have hallucinogenic properties in varying degrees: chloroform, ether, and nitrous oxide.

Although the hallucinogenic agents throughout their long history have served primarily to stimulate religious and spiritual understanding, our interest today in their potential value to humanity has been directed into a number of additional channels. For example, these drugs, particularly LSD, when used as aids in the process of psychotherapy, have been found to be sometimes startlingly effective in releasing blocked emotions, recovering repressed childhood memories, revealing defense mechanisms, and developing emotional insights. These drugs are also helping us study the creativity of professional artists, sculptors, writers, and musicians.

By observing the effects of such drugs, we are gaining a better understanding of the transmission of nerve impulses and the localization of various brain functions. Several of the hallucinogens are being used in both animal and human experimentation to stimulate and then to observe states of fear and anger, to study psychosis, and to investigate the learning processes involved in conditioning and abstract thinking. Some hallucinogens are said to be used in other less humanitarian experiments being carried out in the fields of chemical warfare and prisoner interrogation.

LSD-25 is a semisynthetic drug derived from ergot, a fungus that grows on rye. Its hallucinogenic quality was discovered by chance in 1943 when Dr. A. Hoffman, a chemist working in the Sandoz Pharmaceutical Laboratories in Switzerland, unknowingly absorbed some of it and developed a peculiar dream-like state accompanied by intensely colored fantasies. Since that time, many research workers have explored the physiological and psychological effects of LSD on both animals and humans. To date, over six hundred scientific papers have appeared on the subject. At present the drug is used exclusively for research purposes. It is not available to the public. Even the participants in a research project in which it is being used must be in a hospital setting and under the constant supervision of a well-trained psychiatrist.

We have found that LSD has certain outstanding values which go far beyond those ordinarily sought in psychotherapy. From the standpoint of the development of inner security, its significance seems to be its ability to allow the subject to transcend the usual narrow limitations of his conscious understanding and to become aware of feelings of love and unity with nature of which he could never have dreamed.

This increased awareness has been eagerly sought by many people who have devoted their lives to spiritual development, such as the Christian saints, the yogis in their efforts to transcend the self, and the Buddhist monks in their quest for satori. Sudden mystical experiences have sometimes occurred spontaneously to individuals who were not even seeking such wonder. In the search for enlightenment, a few persons have attained this new state of consciousness by withdrawing into a lonely spot and fasting. Such, in an extraordinarily complete sense, was the experience of Christ in the desert before He began His teaching. Gautama, the Buddha, as he sat under the bodhi tree, was also one of those blessed with a sudden complete and direct realization of life without the intervention of our usual symbolic thought processes.

The experience of such totally comprehensive wisdom, however, has been rare. What has been amazing to those of us experimenting with the hallucinogens has been the apparent ability of many people in all walks of life to have a sudden partial lifting of the veil between what we usually call consciousness and a mental state in which such great unity and completeness is felt that a permanent attitude of optimism toward life may sometimes be crystallized in a moment. Such mystical experiences have not been so prevalent among the volunteers for our experiments that we can expect them routinely. But there seems to be a greater capability in the human being to attain this state, if even for only a moment, than we would have thought possible.

Many subjects have reported religious revelations in which God became a reality. Furthermore, their lives have been significantly and permanently changed by the realization of a kind of divine love which they found within themselves. Many people who have had LSD are unquestionably much more capable of loving than they had been previously. The inability to love is now being recognized as the root of the major tragic sicknesses of our day, whether manifested in international affairs, economics, interpersonal relationships, or psychosomatic illnesses of individuals.

The wonder of LSD is that it can bring within the capabilities of ordinary people the experience of universal love and the reality of our divine nature which was once possible only to the mystics. There are those of us who would like to see the opportunity to experience a series of LSD sessions given to most of the people in positions of influence and leadership, such as teachers, doctors, lawyers, ministers, and politicians. Man's unconscious is a storehouse of his complete range of emotions. These feelings motivate both competition and cooperation. Without subscribing to a Pollyanna attitude, it seems that people have an untapped potential of great love and wisdom which is too often neglected in trying to satisfy the imperious power demands of the ego. It is the release of this innate wisdom and creative energy in people that offers promise of being the greatest benefit to result from the future use of LSD.

Perhaps an analogy can explain the difficulty of communicating the LSD experience. Imagine yourself looking at a beautiful sunset with a friend. It would be possible to communicate your impression of the colors to this companion, but even as you speak, the colors change. To communicate your emotional state at such a time would probably be nearly impossible. When you read Miss Dunlap's minutely described visualizations and insights in the following chapters, you may know that for all her skill in painting word pictures, the true essence of her experiences can never be communicated. It will forever remain as only a vague aura in her personality, perhaps only half conscious to herself.

Although much visual memory of an experience may fade, once a person has been emotionally stirred to such depths, he can never completely lose his new sense of awareness. When the innate wisdom unveiled by LSD has become truly integrated into one's daily life, a vital change takes place in one's relations with other people. An example is the change Miss Dunlap's children recognized in her relationship with them.

After having read the remarkably colorful descriptions of her rich fantasies which culminated in a magnificent religious revelation, I encouraged Miss Dunlap to publish her experiences, partly as a scientific document and partly as an inspiration to people who still believe in the intrinsic spiritual power within the universe. I particularly hoped that her experiences would illustrate the possibilities of this drug's power to expand the consciousness of the already well-integrated individual and those who seek a still deeper wisdom and awareness of a fundamental unity with the life process.

It is typical of the frank, direct approach of Miss Dunlap to describe her fantasies so openly in this book, knowing that they reveal the very depths of her personality. She has presented her experiences just as they occurred. Much of what she had hoped to find through LSD was realized. She was ready for the insights which appeared. She had an unusually rich background of associations through which her spiritual realizations and love feelings could be expressed.

Every LSD experience is unique. That which is perceived is oneself. Since we are all part of life, however, the basic wisdom Jane Dunlap found in herself is the wisdom hidden in the unconscious of each of us. She speaks eloquently for us all.

CHAPTER 1

As Seen Through LSD

THE STACK of *Life* magazines in the corner of the garage had grown a foot or two higher each year, the dust thicker, layer by layer. They were all there, from the very first issue. By the time the children were old enough to use them for school references, I was sick of the sight of them and threw them out. They had served their purpose; few had gone unread.

Of all the excellent articles the magazine had carried, the one which fascinated me most was by Robert Gordon Wasson[1] on the magic mushrooms of Mexico. The mushrooms, he wrote, caused persons eating them to have visions and mystical experiences and for these reasons had been used in religious ceremonies for hundreds, perhaps thousands, of years. He and his wife ate some of the mushrooms, saw beautiful scenes and colors, and felt rich emotions. As I read, I was overcome with an envy which refused to disappear.

When Dr. Snow, a friend of twenty years' standing, mentioned that he was studying the effects of lysergic acid, a cousin to the Mexican mushrooms' magic, I immediately

[1] Wasson, Robert Gordon. "Seeking the Magic Mushroom," *Life*, May 13, 1957.

begged to become an experimental subject. He referred me to the psychiatric department of a nearby university where research was in progress on lysergic acid diethylamide, also known as LSD-25. Unfortunately they were not eager to have me. Far more people had volunteered than could be given the drug. Nevertheless, I pestered them for months.

When research is being done on a drug whose effects are physical, these effects can be studied by measuring the blood pressure, analyzing body fluids, and similar techniques. If the drug affects the mind, however, about the only way its effect can become known is by having hundreds of persons describe what happened to them while under its influence. The problem, therefore, becomes partly one of finding persons capable of writing full and accurate descriptions. Many people find it difficult to express what they have seen and felt. For example, an alcoholic, given LSD, was asked to write a report of his experience. He complied, but it contained only four words: "God, what a binge!"

Probably it was because I am an author that I was eventually allowed to have the drug. On each occasion, I too was asked to write a report the day following the experience, while memories were still fresh. These reports, written as accurately as I could possibly make them, form the next eleven chapters of this book.

Friends interested in LSD have bombarded me with questions, many of which Dr. Davidson has answered in the Introduction and in the Appendix. Since the study of consciousness-changing drugs is certainly not my field, I leave the history of the drug, its derivation, it similarities to better known substances, and its possible uses to him.

People naturally want to know why I wished to take LSD. The fact that related substances were used for religious purposes interested me profoundly, and I had heard that LSD experiences were often deeply spiritual. For many years it has seemed to me that, before any of us can have truly fulfilling lives, we must develop intellectually, physically, emotionally, and spiritually. Intellectual and physical development are tremendously stressed in our culture, perhaps overstressed. Emotional and spiritual development, I feel, are both neglected and underestimated. Through several years of painful but glorious psychoanalysis and psychotherapy, I have done considerable maturing emotionally and laid the foundation for further emotional growth. Intellectually I could have done better but also worse; with greater leisure in the future and night teaching by means of a tape recorder, I trust intellectual development may continue. Physically I can still count my days of illness on my fingers and enjoy daily swimming, frequent ice skating, and a not-too-bad game of badminton, all of which I hope to improve. When it came to spiritual attainment, however, my development was so pitifully inadequate that I sometimes felt consumed with an empty yearning.

Even as a child I believed in God, though I was certainly vague as to Who or What He was. As I grew older, He seemed to be something you felt when walking through the redwoods or watching a colorful sunrise or sunset, a pounding surf, or a tranquil lagoon. Rarely did I feel Him in church despite an attendance record which must be well above average. And I was not convinced that He listened to my prayers, much less answered them.

During my early years I was terrified of a fiery hell; and I half believed in a billowy-clouded, angel-filled, harp-orchestrated heaven which I knew I could never enter. Regardless of how hard I tried to be "good," my life seemed filled with heaven-barring misdemeanors. Of one thing I remained consistently certain: I, myself, would never see God.

Although growth means constant change and development, my belief in God and feelings about Him stayed much the same year after year except that I discarded my concepts of heaven and hell. In short, I was in a spiritual rut; furthermore I had no idea how to get out of it. Frankly I feel that I had a great deal of company and that my rut was really quite crowded. For these reasons, when filling out a questionnaire which asked, "Why do you wish to take lysergic acid?" I wrote: "In hope of overcoming spiritual poverty." Another time I filled the blank with: "To get chemical Christianity."

The often asked question, "Is LSD habit forming?" is quickly answered. Scientists have said and Dr. Davidson reassures us that it is not. I would say it is habit forming in the same way that attending church or going to an art gallery or symphony is. If you have had a wonderfully rewarding experience, you are eager for more. There is, however, no feeling of urgency in wanting the drug again, but rather an attitude that some day I would perhaps enjoy having it another time.

"Are the visions like dreams?" friends have wanted to know. The experiences have been described as waking dreams. But to me, the visions are far more colorful and vivid than any dream can possibly be. You see LSD pictures with striking and unforgettable clarity. The two are similar in that LSD material may be expressed in symbolism, as dreams are, and awareness comes in the same manner in both. For example, if you dream you are falling and simultaneously feel yourself hurtling through space, you neither ask how you knew you were falling nor could you give the answer if someone questioned you. The fact that you were falling, however, probably seemed so convincingly realistic that neither you nor anyone else would doubt your having felt it. All visions and feelings which come when one is under LSD make themselves known in that same startlingly convincing manner.

In all other respects, however, the experiences seem to me much more like going to a movie which is so dramatic and emotionally packed that it claims every instant of your attention. Most visions I have seen have been similar to Technicolor films in that they are in color and move constantly, although there have also been periods of complete darkness. As in a movie, one is usually aware of surroundings, of anyone entering or leaving the room, and of conversation, but these things remain as mere awarenesses. One can talk but rarely desires to do so. Interruptions during an excellent movie, such as children repeatedly squeezing past you, can be annoying. Similarly interruptions during an LSD experience, when feelings are tremendously heightened, may actually become painful. Just as one can have irrelevant thoughts during a movie, such thoughts occur under the drug. In one respect, however, the two are markedly different: except on the day the drug is given, there are no reruns under LSD. The drug takes you into a world no one except yourself can ever enter. Even you can never enter this same world the second time.

In somewhat the same way that no two drivers get identical performance from a certain gasoline, each individual has an entirely different type of experience under the drug. I have no idea what visions Mrs. Smith (housewife), Mr. Jones (truck driver), or Mr. Brown (milkman) might see if they were given LSD, but their hallucinations would be totally unlike mine. The uniqueness of the drug experience depends, in part at least, upon the personality, knowledge, background, and interests of the subject. The degree to which he can allow himself to be carried unresistingly by the tidal waves of visions seems to determine the richness of the experiences. Some persons, given LSD, have markedly unpleasant sessions, suffering perhaps stark horror or terror or becoming violently ill.

Several friends have asked, "How could you possibly remember everything in such detail?"

The entire day after each experience I spent at the typewriter, getting down the material as fast as I could. I happen to have a fairly good memory, which no doubt helped, but to me an LSD experience is so vivid it would be impossible not to have perfect recall. I talked to one girl who had been given the drug five years ago. She remarked, "I think I could tell you about every second of the experience right now and not omit a single detail, but the wonderful feeling of euphoria left after the first month."

People have asked if the experiences are like hypnosis. I would say they are completely dissimilar, although the attitudes toward the two are quite parallel. Many persons are so terrified of letting go that they would not consider either being hypnotized or taking LSD. Other individuals may want to be hypnotized but find it impossible. Similarly some people take LSD but can allow themselves to have almost no reaction to it. Two acquaintances, both of whom took the drug four times, had one glorious experience each and three duds when nothing happened. I was told of a man who, under LSD, gave one mighty belly roar before the curtain fell. The fear of letting go can amount to genuine terror which I suspect is universal. I felt this terror each time I had the drug and even developed it into the theme of the fourth experience.

Besides terror, mild headaches and nausea occurred intermittently with each of my experiences. My muscles often refused to coordinate, and at times it seemed impossible to walk or write. Certainly I could not have driven a car. I was usually comfortable when lying down but weak and shaky if I attempted to rise. When LSD is taken by mouth, it leaves an unpleasant chemical taste, somewhat alleviated by chewing gum. Hunger pangs, exaggerated by the LSD, sometimes become severely painful. Cumulatively the feelings are sufficiently unpleasant to assure that the drug would not be worth taking unless the rewards were great.

One person who read these reports commented, "I can't tell when you're under the drug and when you aren't." The truth of the matter is, I cannot either. Shakespeare's phrase, "One man in his time plays many parts," is amazingly applicable to a person having an LSD experience. It is a little like playing charades except that you are both the observer and the observed, the observed in some cases being a dozen or more different people, animals, or objects. At the same time, rational thoughts may mingle with irrational ones, and to tell which thoughts belong to which character when you are playing every part is confusing indeed. Since all thoughts are influenced by the drug, I have included both the rational and irrational ones and whenever possible have stated which role seemed to do the thinking.

A girl who typed some of the reports remarked, "I find the material fascinating, but I don't believe a word of it."

Although I can understand her feelings, another friend summed up my convictions by saying, "No one has an imagination like that." Actually drug-induced visions are not unknown to us. Many persons have visions when going under certain anesthetics. Delirium tremens, unfortunately, is well known.

Experiences under lysergic acid can be overwhelmingly rich and emotionally kaleidoscopic. They may begin innocently with light incidents or even ridiculous situations and, almost without your knowing it, can lead you into soul-shaking emotions which can be quite disturbing, even to a reader. One person has described them as being "Wagner fortissimo." For this reason, each experience has been divided into two or more chapters. Some persons have found it best to read no more than a chapter at a time and allow at least a day to pass before starting the next.

The consciousness-changing drugs give a glimpse into the mind which to me is fascinating. How many times each day do we tell ourselves we are stupid, as we say the wrong thing, think of that brilliant reply two weeks too late, carelessly knock over an ash tray, or do some other seemingly foolish thing? Since taking the drug and reading other people's reports of their experiences, I stand in awe of this thing we call the mind. What is in my mind, I am convinced, is essentially in yours and in that of every other individual. For this reason the following chapters seem to me to be not merely about myself but about every person who lives. At times LSD taps a universal knowing in much the same way an oil drill may tap a vast underground field which has existed for millions of years. One could almost say lysergic acid gives a glimpse into the very soul of man.

CHAPTER 2

I Lived Billions of Years in Eight Hours

AT LAST the great day, October 24, 1959, arrived. Helen, a close friend of years' standing, was to take LSD with me. We had filled out applications, history sheets, and questionnaires, been interviewed and interrogated, and passed the requirements of physical and mental health. Yet one delay had followed another. The rules were strict: first, a psychiatrist who had done research on LSD had to be with us every minute for eight hours or longer; and second, we had to be in a hospital setting. The university physicians were swamped with work. Dr. Snow, a practicing psychiatrist, had graciously volunteered to be "baby sitter" on his first free Saturday. Although I had phoned him week after week, it had seemed his free Saturday would never come.

Since sensations are tremendously heightened by LSD, it was considered important for us to be in as attractive surroundings as possible. Our "hospital setting," therefore, was to be Dr. Snow's beautiful home rather than the somewhat dreary rooms of the university infirmary where interruptions and traffic noises could disturb us. I visualized us as quietly enjoying our hallucinations while Frank, my husband, watched us. He had done some work with the university group and had been given several consciousness-changing drugs. Dr. Snow would thus be free to read or to write one of his many scientific papers. My feeling was that we would be not the slightest bother to the Snow family.

Immediately after we arrived, Helen and Mrs. Snow selected music and put records on the hi-fi while I visited with Dr. Snow. He is a man of slight build, balding, chipper, with a fine intelligent face and with eyes as quick and alert as a sparrow's. One is so aware of his sympathy and kindness that it is impossible not to love him.

Before ten o'clock the head of the university research group brought the drug and allotted me 110 micrograms which was given to me intramuscularly. Helen, somewhat smaller than I, was given 100 micrograms.

I strolled into the living room and sat down expecting to wait half an hour or longer before anything happened. Furnished as it was in elegant but quiet good taste, it was far more pleasant than any hospital. The carpet, huge sectional davenports, and roomy lounging chairs were all spotlessly off-white. A modern print, many small pillows, and the walls of books on either side of the fireplace gave the room just the right amount of color. Four large French doors led to a vine-covered patio and made the lovely garden and sparkling pool part of the room itself. It was good to be alone here, to think and feel and tremble, for fear was gradually coming over me.

In less than ten minutes after the drug was given me, I felt dizzy. I started to take notes, but my fingers seemed large and refused to coordinate. Helen came in and collapsed in a large chair identical to the one I had chosen. A low table stood between us, and a large white lamp shade hid her face from my view.

Soon I became an angel floating delightfully through space, every cell in my body in a frenzy of joyous vibration. From then on emotions, intensified to the *n*th degree, changed with lightning quickness. Suddenly a choking terror gripped me. I was being carried out as though I were caught in a mad, surging rip tide. I felt utterly helpless, realizing it was impossible to resist such a mighty and powerful force. This blood-freezing emotion, I knew, could be relieved if Dr. Snow, seated near us, would pray for me. Although I asked him to pray and he is a deeply religious man, he was now wholly a psychiatrist and remained silent. I repeated my request, feeling that he simply must comply. There was such an urgency in my need that I dug my fingernails into clenched palms as if to force him to pray. When he still failed to comply, I whispered the Lord's prayer, feeling instantly both a tremendous security and a bitter loathing for Dr. Snow.

Immediately I wanted music, now and not a second later. This time my request was granted, and the music seemed more beautiful than any I had ever heard before. It penetrated every cell of my body, as if each cell had become an auditory nerve. The recording was an instrumental one of several pieces: the first, *None but the Lonely Heart.*

"Loneliness is universal," I thought. "Every person who has ever lived or is alive has suffered loneliness."

For a fleeting moment I was each individual, and a second later a composite of all individuals who live or had lived, suffering the sum total of all loneliness and crying out in torturous agony.

"Can know my sadness."

The music was in itself unbelievably sad. I suffered what seemed to be all the sadness the world had ever known, sobbing loudly and writhing with this unbearable burden which tore me apart. I wanted desperately to read Edna St. Vincent Millay's *Renascence*, thinking especially of the passage:

> *I saw at sea a great fog-bank*
> *Between two ships that struck and sank;*
> *A thousand screams the heavens smote;*
> *And every scream tore through my throat.*
> *No hurt I did not feel, no death*
> *That was not mine; mine each last breath*
> *That, crying, met an answering cry*
> *From the compassion that was I.*

She had experienced some of the agony I was experiencing; she had suffered for all as I was suffering. My longing to read the entire poem was so intense I asked Dr. Snow to locate a copy. I could hear him and Mrs. Snow moving quickly about for what seemed an eternity before he threw me into bitter disappointment by reporting they had been unsuccessful.

Then came inconceivably beautiful strains of *Ave Maria*, its loveliness bringing torrents of tears. The Blessed Holy Mother had comforted the suffering, had eased the world's sadness and loneliness. I was filled with love, the Holy Mother's love and all the love the world had ever known, infinitely more painful than either loneliness or sadness had been. It seemed as if every cell in my body was sobbing separately, as if every person who lives or had lived was sobbing in me and with me. When such pain could not be borne another second, I was again an angel ascending to heaven, beautiful wings outstretched, each covered with thousands of perfect feathers of purest white, overlapping with absolute symmetry. Although the music continued throughout the day, I did not hear another note of the recordings.

The scene shifted with inconceivable swiftness. Before me

were pictures of Dante's *Inferno* and large Biblical pictures depicting hell: writhing people and beasts trying to escape floods, flames, and snakes. These pictures became a composite of hundreds of similar pictures, each filled with writhing, tortured, intertwined humanity, reptiles, and beasts. Then I became each terrorized, tortured human and beast, writhing in death which was continuous and eternal, without the relief of dying. These vividly clear scenes, like all later ones, appeared to be only incidental props upon which were hung the most violent of emotions.

Until five o'clock that evening, with scarcely a moment's relief, I writhed with some kind of torture, making loud noises which I was powerless to prevent. Overwhelming sensations were seemingly continuous with no letup, although there were moments of semiclarity. My throat and jaw muscles often felt knotted and stiff as if made of steel, and at times there was painful pressure inside my ears.

When I had started to sob, Dr. Snow had moved a chair beside me and put a box of facial tissue on it, an act which seemed the sum total of all human kindness. By this one act, he seemed to have given me everything I had ever wanted. Frank had come into the room, and both he and Dr. Snow appeared to be wonderful, God-like creatures whom I loved as I had never loved before. I had not known one could love with such intensity. Their presence gave me a momentary but wonderful feeling of security.

I was aware that my thinking processes were working more rapidly and clearly than ever before. A window across the room seemed to be a cathedral window of marvelous stained glass; a picture I had painted seemed larger than it actually was but of no earthly importance. Of these things I was merely aware. It was the stark and amazing reality of non-reality which claimed all my attention, each vivid scene blending into the next with lightning speed, like a movie run many times too fast.

After the multiple writhings and tortures of hell, I was left in blackness, and it seemed impossible for me to get my breath. I was gasping, breathing harder than I had breathed before. Then clarity came, and I was the first fish ever to be on land, fighting for my life; the pond where I had lived had dried up. Soon I was all the fish which had lived where water had dried up. Hot arid winds blew over me. The earth was rocky and mustard yellow, and no living plant could be seen. Millions upon millions of us lay dying until every fish on land had died. I collapsed in agonized "death" and scarcely breathed at all.

In the meantime Dr. Snow, who had been watching me intently, had become alarmed at my hard breathing. I was aware of his coming to me and was annoyed by the interruption. Later he said he had asked me to breathe into a paper bag and to rebreathe the carbon dioxide, thus preventing alkalosis, but I neither heard his request nor saw the bag. The hallucinations were so convincing and all absorbing that I, as a person, seemed to have completely ceased to exist.

When "I" recovered from "death," the ocean was lapping the shore near me, bringing tiny shells and single-celled and few-celled animals. I was a one-celled ameba, throbbing like a heartbeat. With a feeling as if I were bursting, my single cell multiplied into millions until I became not only all near-microscopic ocean life which learned to live on land but also small lichen clinging to bare rocks.

I was the first tiny seed bursting and pushing, with infinite difficulty and every cell in my body, through the rocky soil; then millions of bursting seeds struggling to send up shoots. I was a single root, trying to force my way around rocks, but found the way inconceivably hard. Quickly I was all roots, forcing, forcing, forcing both downward and laterally so that life above could live. Next I became the first plant, a single tiny shoot with a green tip. The shoot was beautiful growing out of the rocky, mustard-colored land, and its lovely green tip became *hope* which gave me, as the beginning of all life, courage to struggle on.

Above me there appeared a light, a tiny sun the size of a star. As all plant and animal life, I was struggling and struggling to reach it, my arms so outstretched as to feel pulled from the shoulder sockets. That little light was God. I must reach Him! I must! I must!

The struggle to live was constant and ever present in each plant and animal. The struggle to reach God was also constant and ever present in each, and infinitely more difficult. This life force was a living thing which throbbed inside every cell, whether plant or animal, and knew no satisfying. Despite the infinite difficulty of these struggles, I had scarcely started populating the earth with few-celled animals and covering its surface with lichens, fungi, and tiny shoots when world-shaking earthquakes came, instantly followed by tremendous waves. My voice became the thunderous rumble of the gigantic quakes and the swishing roar of the fierce waves which beat and overran the sad land, the shaking and beating almost tearing my body apart. Life on land was destroyed—my life and all of my lives. I sobbed uncontrollably at such heedless and cruel destruction.

Again I collapsed into lethargy. Yet I could hear Helen repeating in a gentle near whisper totally unlike her natural voice: "There never was such a beautiful world, such a beautiful world."

Soon I became with lightning sequence a single cell, lichen, seeds, roots, shoots, and an ugly little amphibian. By this time I was lying on the floor, a rocky shore. With tremendous difficulty I attempted to climb over the rocks, but my short, almost useless front legs, which were the upper part of my arms, felt weak and extremely painful. Though I tried to hold up my head, my neck too was weak, uncomfortable, and rigidly stiff. But I was on land, and I could live on land. Despite the struggles, I had made it. I felt proudly victorious.

In an instant millions of years had passed, and the earth was filled with every type of prehistoric animal: snakes, lizards, crocodile-like beasts, dinosaurs, and amphibians and reptiles of every sort and size, all fighting in green marshes luxuriant with tropical growth. Seemingly I became each of these beasts, one by one, all making loud and continuous noises and all fiercely fighting in death struggles, consumed with hatred and terror. I knew I must kill instantly or else be killed. To kill immediately was my only means of survival. To kill for food was merely incidental. Each animal which attacked me seemed more terrifying than the previous one. All, in their rage and ferocity, were ugly beyond description. Their hatred was a seething, poisonous reptile in itself. Their terror was a gripping, choking thing, horrible in its aliveness. It tore me with sobs and seemed to shrink every cell in my body, freezing my blood to ice.

For a time I was a hideously ugly beast about six feet in length, with a short, alligator-like body, a long neck, and a head like a huge snake. With my feet in squashy slime and my long, narrow tongue quickly extending with each hiss, I stood hating, hissing, attacking, my own tongue extending and my body lurching.

Repeatedly I was lizards, phytosaurs, and snakes, fighting my way through reeds or thick mud or over rocks. Between blinding splashes of muddy water and green slime, I could see a great tangle of trampled ferns, lunging bodies, and the kicking, gurgling, dying animals, their moist brown, gray, or black hides and bony plates shining in the sun. I could feel the powerful impact of great, crocodile-like tails slashing at me and the jabbing, razor-sharp teeth sink with vise-like grip into my throat, then hear my death gurgles as I sank into the mire. For hours I hissed and snarled, bit and fought to preserve my composite life of thousands of animals. With each individually I fought, first a hiss, then a lunge, a snarl, a bite, a death gurgle, my mouth foaming, and my body, arms, and legs threshing in every direction. At the same time I was sobbing with terror and overcome by the horror before me. The pile of used facial tissues by my side quickly grew to hill proportions.

For a moment I was Brontosaurus rex, king of the dinosaurs, standing in muddy water three or four feet deep and surrounded with other dinosaurs of every kind; my legs felt inconceivably heavy, my body unbearably cumbersome. Then I was all dinosaurs; as each one of them, too, I was fighting, swinging tremendous tails, gouging with bony plates, shoving tons of flesh against tons of flesh, falling heavily among the reeds, and writhing in miserable death throes, my body going through every motion with them.

I was many kinds of prehistoric birds with black bat-like wings and long, thin wing bones, flying awkwardly into low branches of stunted, palm-like trees, fighting on land and in air and diving for animals below, squawking raucously all the while.

Again and again I was a great muddy tangle of lizards, birds, dinosaurs, alligator-like beasts, and snakes, striking, lunging, biting, hitting, hissing, and lashing out with great tails. As millions of animals I died; as a few I survived.

"This is why we have wars," I thought. "Life has been an unending struggle and fight since time began." Repeatedly I asked myself, "How *could* man ever have evolved from this?"

As if in answer, there appeared before me the sun that was God, the size of a small moon this time. I realized that God had made Himself felt as the life force which had demanded evolution. I, as every prehistoric animal, had felt this life force as a restless driving which had been so great as to supersede even terror and hatred. It was this force, this will to survive, which had caused me to fight with such ferocity, to hate my enemies, and to be terrified of being destroyed.

The noises I had been emitting amazed me by sounding completely realistic. At that time I was even convinced I could be tremendously successful as a "sound effects man" on any movie set. Frank's notes state simply, "Jane continues to make loud animal noises; writhes clockwise for two or three revolutions, then counterwise," followed in half-hour intervals by ditto marks. At this stage, of course, neither Helen nor I knew what the other was experiencing. She was deep in a world where color became magnificent music and music became beautiful colors and designs, a world in which nothing inharmonious could enter. Later she stated repeatedly that my noises had nothing to do with me. Whether by telepathy or as a tribute to my LSD acting, her report, written that night before she went to bed, contained the following:

"Outside my world I could hear a discordant cacophony of snarls and hisses, wails and growls. I felt the presence of a primordial forest with the struggle of animal and reptilian life in ooze and slime and lush tropical growth. The hideously discordant sounds became harmonious and took on symmetry and beauty of form, color, and movement, blending into my symphony of radiance and sound. Throughout my experience she was not Jane but the actual forms of life her sounds portrayed."

Later Helen unflatteringly said my noise sounded somewhat like that of cats breeding at night directly under the bedroom window. For me, however, the situation contained neither humor nor make-believe but only stark and terrifying reality.

Without the slightest interruption, I changed from being dying animals to becoming hundreds of volcanic eruptions, my internal pressures forcing fiery lava miles into the sky. I was thousands of animals slithering, lunging, and fleeing in panic before rivers of molten lava, a brilliant red glow lighting the whole of the heavens. The torturous multiple-death writhings of all the animals were mine. I howled with their unbearable pain and felt myself both freeze with terror and burned like strips of bacon tossed into flames. The pain of being burned was so real that for a moment I wanted all the ointments the world had ever produced.

Quickly I became great rivers of lava which poured hissing into the sea. I hissed loudly, my hissing different now from that of the tough-bellied lizards and snakes. Somehow I was all the animals still alive after the volcanic eruptions, fighting to breathe ash-filled air in perpetual midnight blackness, suffocating, dying. Still I lived as thousands of other animals, searching desperately for food after all plants had been killed, coughing as I tried to drink acrid, ash-thick water, then dying of thirst and starvation. As few species, I survived on an earth no sun could reach for so many centuries that an ice age formed. I, as a symbol of all life, seemed to die hopelessly on a bleak and frozen earth.

As the chemically induced charades continued, I became howling blizzards, glaciers of crushing weight, and a gouged and tumbling earth. My voice became the sound of the wind, and my body, the heavy, shoving glaciers and the disheveled ground. Since all life had been utterly destroyed, I lay inert in "death," sobbing at such sheer desolation, such stark defeat. Eons passed. Then I was again an ameba, still pulsating like a rapid heartbeat, the beautiful green-tipped shoot, the weak-necked little amphibian, and finally again the thousands of animals struggling together, snarling, biting, clawing, hissing, lunging, killing.

My noises were finally wearing Helen down. In a soft but pleading voice, she cried, "Peace, give me peace."

Quick as lightning and without forethought came my emphatic answer: "There is no peace! There is no peace!"

Helen's report of my answer reads: "All the primordial animals beside my world snarled in reply."

Immediately I was back viewing the struggle for survival. "How *could* man have come from this?" I cried. Again there came the light that was both God and the sun, now the size of a full moon. Somehow, as every planet or animal, I had to reach it; no amount of struggle was a price too great.

Millions more years passed. Around me was a jungle, huge trees shading a tangle of luxuriant growth, brilliant flowers, and mottled bits of sunshine on a damp earth. In the distance I could see gently sloping plains broken by lakes and rivers. For a moment I was a graceful gazelle, loping over the plains; a huge lion, secure and at peace in the sun; long, beautiful snakes, slithering this time through thickets of grass; myriads of vultures, diving for prey, proud of my function as garbage-disposal squad; a great scorpion, pressing my buttocks to sting my next meal; a black panther, tearing still-warm meat from bones; every manner of fowl, migrating to the north for breeding; a mother duck swimming among the reeds, a brood of fuzzy ducklings following me; birds with brilliant plumage, chattering in tropical forests; a leopardess with my cubs, then each of the cubs, spitting at anything which frightened me. This scene, like all the others, recurred again and again, and each time I, as a cub, started spitting I burst out laughing, the only part of the entire experience which seemed amusing.

In sequence I was every animal of every jungle and every plain on every continent: zebras, monkeys, reptiles, crocodiles, many varieties of cats and antelopes, and hundreds of others. As each the life force, that urge to reach the sun and God, that ceaseless drive to evolve, was hot within my breast. Then as in the marshes, I, as the animals of plains and jungles, was fighting, snarling, clawing, biting, stinging, hissing. With each I growled, snarled, clawed, bit, stung, killed, and was killed. As each of the weak, I died; as few of the fittest I survived.

This time there seemed to be a nobility in my fighting. Cruelty there certainly was, but I did not fight to be cruel. I fought only to survive, either to keep from being destroyed or to obtain food. There seemed nothing wrong with this kind of fighting. As the animals of the jungles and plains, I felt very different from those in the marshes. Terror was not so ever present. As the mother duck and the leopardess, I felt the rudiments of love and protectiveness. As lion, snake, and panther, I knew a degree of security; as fowl, a sense of freedom; as monkey and antelope, a joy in rhythm of movement and something kindred to a desire for peace. It seemed wonderful to me that positive emotions were beginning to evolve.

Then as my body went through a long series of fantastic motions, I became the north wind whipping blizzards across the plains and animals freezing to death; rain pouring in torrents, bringing floods which destroyed much of life; hundreds of volcanoes, burning alike tortured earth and beasts; the earth convulsed with quakes; majestic mountains formed by the convulsions; mighty waves dashing on the beaches; glaciers of other ice ages; thunder roaring and lightning splitting the heavens. Immediately I was great forest fires set by the lightning, flames leaping high into the sky and roaring before the wind; terrified animals fleeing from the fires, overcome by smoke and flames, coughing as if my lungs were being destroyed, then dying agonized deaths; and finally the charred stumps and the brown, burned earth. In a geological split second I was billions of bursting seeds which instantly covered the earth with rank growth, leaving only blackened tree trunks to show there had been fire. Again and again, as millenniums sped by, I was the death of all things, the rebirth of all things. Many times during each million-year span, I, as the sum total of the animals of plains and jungles, seemed doomed to extinction. The struggle made by the few which lived seemed incomprehensible.

Despite the fact that the kaleidoscopic shifting of vivid scenes and violent emotions seemed to demand the attention of every brain cell, I found myself wanting to tell Frank and Dr. Snow what I was experiencing. At intervals I would exclaim: "I am all of evolution, every bit of it"; "No one could write a report on this; you would have to write an encyclopedia"; "I'm not all things to all men; I'm all things to all things." When experiencing the ferocity of fighting in swamps or jungles, I felt overcome with awe, repeating again and again, "How *could* man have evolved from this?" It seemed so utterly impossible that I knew even then there was only one answer: evolution was the handiwork of God.

Suddenly I wanted to vomit, immediately and with violence. I ran to a door, Frank springing to help me; but he would not let me out. I ran to another door; still he would not let me out. Only later did I understand that all doors had been locked and the keys removed. I felt that I would vomit immediately all over the white living-room carpet and that the vomitus would inundate the house. Millions of years seemed to pass before Dr. Snow came with the key, and the door was finally opened. I ran into the garden, retching as I went. Although only a little saliva came, I was convinced a great river of vomitus was pouring from my mouth. I threw myself on the grass, "vomiting" again and again. During this sequence, I felt I was the sum total of all humanity. What meaning, if any, such feelings contained, I neither knew nor cared.

At last the miserable retching stopped, and the beauty of the garden pressed in against me. It was as though the terror, pain, hideousness, destruction, and death I had both experienced and witnessed had combined into a tremendous bulldozer which had dug a vast pit now filling with a lake of peaceful bliss. Sobs of relief and gratitude shook my body and tore at my soul to even greater depths than had either pain or terror.

CHAPTER 3

The Evolution of the Soul

THE LOUD and hideous cacophony of sounds which poured from my throat hour after hour caused me, during flashes of clarity, to writhe with embarrassment, shame, and remorse, all too keenly aware of how blatantly I had intruded on Dr. Snow's one day at home. Though it was nearly midafternoon, neither he nor Frank had had a minute to eat lunch. Furthermore, since I insisted on being out of doors and Frank had seated himself beside me, Dr. Snow was forced to spend every minute watching Helen. I also regretted that his young son, a potential interruption, had been sent away from home for the day and that Mrs. Snow, who had been taking a course at the university, was trying to study for an examination. How could she concentrate beside a primordial swamp of struggling beasts?

As soon as I had thrown myself on the grass, Dr. Snow brought a rug for me to lie on. Since grass was a familiar part of my marshes and jungles, I spurned it. I did become vaguely aware that he was telling me that I had to keep quiet because of the neighbors. Although with difficulty I subdued my hissing and growling somewhat, it is only by the miracle of Christianity on their part that I am still friends with the Snows.

The scenes which must have been repeated twenty or more times again passed before me: the throbbing ameba; the tiny green-tipped *hope;* the brave little amphibian; the catastrophes; and the tangle of snarling, hissing, lunging animals fighting in marshes and jungles. Although every detail was complete in each repetition, the scenes shifted more rapidly and the duration of each agony became increasingly less. Invariably the terror and fighting left me sobbing, but now I could grab Frank's hand to ease the pain. His presence and silence were comforting, and I was grateful that he too had had LSD.

Like the English ballad, *The Twelve Days of Christmas,* something new was added with each repetition of the beginnings of evolution. This time I was a kangaroo with a baby in my pouch, fleeing from an enemy; I was the baby, peeking out at a blurred, rapidly moving world; a lone wolf, howling into a winter night; a white fox, slinking across beautifully molded snowdrifts; a starved weasel in white winter coat, searching desperately for food; a whale, noisily spouting tremendous fountains; walrus and seal playing in icy waters; and the aurora borealis dancing in the heavens. Fortunately I was also myself viewing the brilliant, darting blues, purples, reds, and oranges which covered the frigid sky. But I was not myself, nor could I care less. Again I was every variety of disaster, every dying plant and beast, lashing, writhing, hissing, sobbing, vomiting, dying. Thus passed millions more years.

Whenever life seemed threatened with annihilation, the light which was God and the sun reappeared, each time a little larger. As every living thing, I felt the urgency to reach it. This restless, driving, throbbing force remained always as great as before, but the possibility of reaching God seemed a little nearer each time. I now knew beyond all doubting that this urge was responsible for evolution.

In what seemed billions of years since the first ameba washed up on shore, I was a caveman, cringing in darkness against a back wall of a cavern. I felt insignificantly small and as terrified as were the prehistoric animals. Then I was all cavemen, leading lives of utter misery. For a moment I was a Cro-Magnon, carving on cave walls, somewhat less frightened now. Then eons sped by, and I was primitive men of every sort: a lake dweller living in a flimsy hut built on stilts, my surroundings so vivid that I could hear the lapping of the blue water which sparkled in the sun; a brown-skinned woman near a grass-hut village in a gloomy tropical forest; an Australian bushman, throwing a javelin across an arid countryside; a cliff dweller, with a hubbub of children playing around me and women grinding corn with pestle and mortar, myself looking out across what is now Arizona and New Mexico; an Eskimo eating frozen meat in an igloo; a nomad roaming, with other nomads, the forests and plains of early Europe and Asia Minor, driving our herds before us. As each, I felt the restless, driving, God force which knew no quieting. As each, I was terrified of the elements, ferocious animals, starvation, sickness, and other tribes; and the fighting continued as in the marshes and jungles. Yet I felt in awe that, out of the struggles and catastrophes of prehistoric life, anything as wonderful as primitive man had managed to survive and evolve.

At this point I walked shakily, with much help from Frank, to a powder room with a mirror wall. A return to the marshes came over me, and in semicoma I watched a grotesque face go through weird contortions. This flexible rubber face had nothing to do with me. As it emitted growls, the mouth stretched far to the right and all but disappeared around the angle of the chin; hisses pulled the mouth upward and to the left; and the forehead, as wrinkled as a bulldog puppy's, compressed in rhythm to other fierce noises.

As soon as I was lying on the grass once more, I became aware of birds singing in the trees above me, their songs inconceivably beautiful. As catastrophe after catastrophe—blizzards, volcanic eruptions, starvation, floods, sickness, forest fires, fighting—all but destroyed man, the bird songs seemed to give promise of something better to come.

Then I became every variety of more highly evolved man, feeling with astonishing keenness and even accuracy, I suspect, what each must have felt. I was a tiny black baby, happily nursing at a pendulous breast; its mother, holding the infant with exquisite tenderness; a Chinese coolie, hunger gnawing at my guts; a pre-science scientist, immensely proud to be the first to discover that babies resulted from intercourse; a Korean woman with aching back, weeding a rice paddy; a fat Turkish sultan, sitting crosslegged, arrogant and cruel; the scantily veiled girls of the harem, sensuous, beautiful, yet cringing with fear; Nero's slave girls being fed to the eels, writhing with the terror and pain they must have suffered; and finally Nero himself, playing an A.D. 64 variety of bop, both indifferent to my surroundings and glorying in the fact that thousands of people I hated were being burned to death.

That evening as Helen, Frank, and I sat in a restaurant discussing our experiences under LSD, short waves of the drug frequently returned. Helen conducted herself like a lady except for tinkly outbursts of unnatural laughter, but my voice kept getting out of control. With vigorous gestures, I enacted the part of Nero as he fiddled, describing the conflagration of Rome in such a piercing voice that our waiter apparently believed me to be drunk.

In the experience itself, however, I passed quickly from Nero to become Socrates, feeling that to die was as nothing compared to forsaking a principle; then Plato, writing my dialogues; Scheherazade, spinning my endless tales; a Moslem, worshiping Allah; then all devout followers of Mohammed, Buddha, and Confucius; Henry VIII, gnawing meat from a bone and casually ordering a henchman to behead my current wife; the miserable wife being beheaded; a monk in a cold, barren cell, copying a manuscript; a single wolf, howling into a snowy night, now a symbol of universal loneliness; and one moment, Cleopatra, sensuous, beautiful, experiencing orgasmic ecstasy, and the next moment, dismally despondent, holding an asp to my breast.

As a composite of thousands of persons who lived during the Middle Ages, I died of cholera, the plague, the Black Death, leprosy, and hundreds of other diseases. Simultaneously I cared for the dying and mourned the dead, thinking, as I sobbed heartbrokenly, that one body could not endure such intensity of pain. I was all murderers and all murdered, all hangmen and all hanged, all lovers and all beloved. I was all beggars, palms outstretched and bodies emaciated, miserable and wretched; all givers of alms, arrogant and disdainful; all galley slaves, their breaking backs feeling the lash of the whip; their driver, glorying in my cruelty; all slave dealers and hunters, bringing back my quarry bound in ropes; all slaves, packed in the filth of stinking ships. There seemed no end either to the props upon which violent emotions were hung or to the variety of intense feelings which pulled me first in one direction and then another.

Next I became Michelangelo, lying wearily on my back while putting the finishing touches to the Sistine Chapel, my arms and shoulders aching; Leonardo da Vinci, hot, dust-covered, pounding a chisel on a block of white marble; sea monsters, threatening every sailor; Columbus, watching the fires on shore, proud and thrilled. I was the Mayans, building their temples; the terrified Mayan virgins, being sacrificed; Navajos, dancing in frenzy around a sand painting; and the warriors of Polovitzski, riding like demons across the plains. Again and again I was tremendous dragons, spitting flames, and other dragons with huge nostrils, snorting smoke rings like huge foot-wide doughnuts.

Without an instant's relief for my tiring brain and body, I became mountain climbers falling to my death; gentle St. Bernards, carrying rescue kits; a sobbing Chinese mother, feeding her children mud during a famine; each of hundreds of people celebrating the rites of spring by having sexual orgies in the fields to bring fertility; vultures, flying over the funeral pyres in India; a Hindu widow, being burned alive with the corpse of my husband. I was each of the 70,000 men killed in the Battle of Gettysburg and yet each member of the surviving families, prostrate with grief; Englishmen, rotting in debtors' prison, filled with despair; all serfs, eking out a starved existence and suffering hunger pains torturously real; all feudal lords, secure behind their moats, collecting taxes of grain; Circe, contemptuously changing my lovers into swine, and the proud and haughty Ulysses, conquering her; the sirens, luring sailors to their deaths, and the dying sailors, unable to resist their songs; young sheiks, riding spirited horses across the Sahara; and chocolate-eyed Moslem maidens, their faces veiled with flimsy white gauze. All of these persons and more I was many, many times, and each reliving caused me to sob in anguish with the terrified, the sick, and the dying.

Abruptly, instead of raw ugliness, sheer beauty lay before

me. I was Toscanini, conducting an orchestra of hundreds of instruments in a concert hall of the sky, my musicians seated on a huge, opalescent cloud which sparkled with diamonds. At the same time, I was the millions of ears of humanity, listening to the first tender strains of the celestial music which rose in crescendo until it saturated my being and absorbed me, egoless, into itself. Somehow in its strains were such qualities as goodness, compassion, and love. I felt one must follow this music as the children followed the Pied Piper. Then it came to me that this Pied Piper was God.

For a few minutes, I seemed to be my normal self again. During this period, Helen walked slowly across the garden and sat on a bench near the pool. To me she appeared to be a small, hurt child of perhaps two. Frank was called away for a moment and asked me to watch her. It seemed as though he had given me an unbearable responsibility, and I feared she might jump into the pool. Despite the fact that she is an excellent swimmer, I was then convinced she was unable to swim and might drown. Frank's quick return brought me unbelievable relief. Later Helen told us that at the time she had actually been reliving an unhappy part of her early childhood, when she had not yet learned to swim; and that she had had a compulsive urge to jump into the water, "to become part of it and blend with it." Such instances of telepathy appear to be common during LSD experiences.

Soon I was again a great variety of persons, lost in a gamut of intense emotions. This time it occurred to me that each of them had experienced the same feelings, struggles, and victories as had the animals in the marshes and jungles. Ever present had been the pull of the life force. This inborn urge to reach God had caused man to evolve until he was capable of love and other positive emotions, a recurring thought which invariably left me overcome with awe.

Repeatedly I told myself, "Never again will I criticize another human being. Every person tries so hard, and there is such courage, such nobility in the trying. But the struggle for survival continues, the grief, sorrow, sadness, terror, loneliness, and killing. The weak fall by the wayside; the strong survive."

Suddenly I felt overcome with compassion. An instant later I became Mary, filled with joy and peace as I rode beside Joseph toward Bethlehem. I was the wise men, bearing gifts, and the shepherds gazing at the star, more brilliant than anything I had ever before seen. We left our flocks and, walking over crackling snow, followed the star; as each of the three, the joy of being with the infant Jesus tore my body with shaking sobs. I was with the child Jesus in the temple, followed Him with His disciples, and with joy in my heart, waved a palm branch as He entered Jerusalem.

Then I was Jesus, hanging on the cross, felt excruciating pain as nails pierced living flesh, and uttered His words, "Father, forgive them; for they know not what they do." As Mary, I sobbed at the foot of the cross. Then He died, was buried, and lived again.

Suddenly His resurrection seemed shockingly unimportant. It was the same story already told thousands of times. *Always after death there had been life.* "The fact that He rose from the dead is considered important," I concluded, "only because we have forgotten what each of us really knows deep inside: all life dies and lives again."

The violent nausea recurred, and I felt that a great river of vomitus the size of the Amazon was gushing through my mouth. It contained the flushings of every toilet of an entire metropolis. Its revolting taste and odor overpowered me, and the retchings seemed to tear my stomach apart. Yet I could not "vomit" enough or in great enough volume. When exhausted, I became the amphibian again, his legs pitifully weak, his neck painfully stiff. By now I was fond of this courageous little lizard, squashy, soft, and ugly though he was. Then came more retching, the great river of vomitus seeming to fall from the height and with the force of Niagara and as continuously as the Niagara flows into Lake Ontario.

At this point the most intense suffering of the entire experience occurred, during every instant of which I writhed in inconceivable agony. I felt I was insane, without hope of recovery. Then I was the sum total of all insane persons who live or have lived. I was thrown into medieval dungeons, savagely treated for possessing "evil spirits," hidden by shame-torn families in back rooms and attics. I writhed in all the snake pits the world has ever known, in irons and strait jackets, suffering the abuse of sadistic attendants, which was mild compared with the mental agonies of the truly damned. I was all incontinent idiots babbling in infinite confusion, all imbeciles and all morons. The suffering was so intense that I exclaimed repeatedly between agonized sobs, "I wouldn't take LSD again for all the gold in Fort Knox," and "This drug isn't habit-forming! No one would take it a second time!"

Dr. Snow was standing beside me, a bottle of tablets in his hand. "If I give you one of these, you'll be completely normal in five minutes."

To my own surprise, I vehemently refused.

Instantly I was back in prehistoric mire, snarling, biting, and hissing. At this point two members of the university research staff came to check on our progress. I was not only annoyed by their interruption but overcome with rage. These marshes were mine, and I would tolerate no intruders. Then I was vaguely aware that someone was introducing one of the men to me, but at that moment there was a final reappearance of my beloved little amphibian. "How ridiculous to be so formal when introducing a person to a lizard," I remarked contemptuously under my breath. After their withdrawal, the experience lost none of its intensity, but the periods of clarity between waves became longer.

The Niagara of vomitus returned, but this time it brought tremendous relief. Then suddenly the trees, shrubs, flowers, lawn, and the nearby pool took on transcendent beauty such as could be created only by the great Painter at His superb excellence, viewed through eyes capable of infinite appreciation. The symphonies of the birds became exaggerated harmony and sweetness, their soft songs touching some kindred melody within me. Every cell of my body became saturated with peace, tranquillity, wonderment, and awe. The whole combined into a joy so intense that it changed to excruciating pain, and I wanted to cry and cry forever. Yet I was in paradise, and my sobs were those of extreme joy. Soon my tears expressed ardent gratitude that paradise had been shown me and that somewhere deep within myself there had hidden this heaven now being revealed.

For a long time I lay watching, listening, weeping, and loving God and everything He had created. I saw the tiny grasses bend in prayer, the flowers dance in the breeze, and the trees lift their arms to God. I heard the water sing in its lapping, the leaves of the shrubs whispering, the soft footsteps of insects hurrying, and the wings of butterflies fluttering. While the harmony, tranquillity, and loveliness of this paradise filled me to overflowing, millions of years were passing.

Gradually I returned to reality and realized it would soon be evening. The entire experience caused me to be overcome with awe and amazement, and I lay on the grass wondering why I had selected such a theme as evolution. The subject had never interested me particularly. I had not taken college courses which dealt with such material or read Darwin or any other book about the evolvement of man. Even if I had read all the books written on the subject, they could not have engrained in me the violent emotions I had experienced.

Then the answer flashed into my mind. That very morning as Frank was backing the car out of the garage, I had flipped quickly through a magazine, and for a second my glance had fallen on the title of an article by Jimmy Michener[2]: "Violence and the Whims of Nature over Millions of Years Built a Paradise." Now I knew that second had influenced the day and, I suspected, all the days I have yet to live. I had both seen and been the violence and whims of nature; I had watched the passing of the millions of years and had arrived at paradise.

Now with sadness I feared the drug had worn itself out; yet I longed to be back in paradise. Despite the suffering, I already dreaded the return to a circumscribed world. Perhaps half an hour later Dr. Snow brought out a tray of cheeses, crackers, milk, and fruits. Mrs. Snow joined us, and we sat in the gathering dusk discussing what Helen and I had seen and felt.

Then the drug swept me once more from the shores of reality. During this final period, the most meaningful part of the day occurred, bringing clarity and summation to the whole. It caused the entire experience to become a deeply religious one, left convictions which plowed furrows of permanence into my very soul, and resulted in my being so overcome with awe and reverence that it was difficult to talk for some time afterward.

Again I was in paradise, but this time I was no more myself than when I, as Brontosaurus rex, had stood belly deep

[2] Michener, James A. *Life*, October 26, 1959.

in slime. I seemed to be any person who had ever lived, a nameless representative of humanity, and yet a composite of all persons. Then with an awe which was almost overpowering, I had a momentary glimpse of what man would eventually evolve into, of the heights he would sometime reach, and of development as yet unimagined. For the most part, that glimpse will forever remain indescribable.

In this stage of evolution which far surpassed that of my actual self, serenity, tranquillity, and joy continuously enfolded me. In addition, my thoughts became crystal clear, flowing quickly, yet as gently as a moving stream. There came a knowing beyond all doubting, convictions unshakable in their strength, as if LSD had pulled back a curtain and allowed the light of wisdom to shine through. In this glorious land, it was as St. Paul had written: I could see "face to face" and "understand fully."

At last I comprehended how "death is swallowed up in victory." I knew that the thousands of deaths I had experienced, each followed by inevitable resurrection, had led me to this paradise, and that these deaths had actually demonstrated deathlessness. I could see that my own death and everyone else's death would eventually be thus victorious.

A kindred conviction came, too strong for argument: time does not exist. We are living in eternity, an eternity which has always been and always will be. Although millions upon millions of years had seemed to be passing, I now knew these eons were but the ticking of the clock of endless time.

Dr. Jung's belief that every person retains race memories came into my mind. Although I had formerly held a perhaps-so-what attitude toward the theory, to me it was now fact. Indeed it could be none other than true; the thousands of feelings I had experienced could not have been contained in a bit of drug smaller than a grain of sugar. Nor had they been gained from my life experiences. Emotions cannot be learned from reading books or attending schools or church services. Furthermore I was convinced that race memories are retained by every person; and that it was these remembered emotions which all too frequently show themselves in what we recognize only as crimes and wars.

I became aware that my violent "vomiting" had been symbolic of the entire human race trying to rid itself of the negative emotions of the marshes. Because of man's ability thus to throw out negative feelings, from the snarling, hissing, and fighting, the catastrophes and the suffering, he had evolved to become capable of such positive emotions as forgiveness, compassion, kindness, mercy, honor, charity, self-sacrifice, and love. From the mud had grown the beauty of the water lily. I felt that most of the insanity I had experienced so devastatingly had resulted from the failure both to pour out these negative emotions and to accept the positive ones.

Another conviction quickly arose: it was that each positive emotion and its negative antithesis indeed constitute one quality rather than two; that just as a coin has two inseparable sides, so are the negative and positive emotions inseparable. I saw clearly that in the same way the dark colors in a painting give beauty and contrast to the pastels, the negative emotions are equally necessary to give depth and meaning to the positive ones; that one could not truly appreciate love without first knowing hate, or beauty without having seen ugliness, or any positive emotion without awareness of its antithesis. I could see that the negative emotion is the salt which gives flavor to the bread; and that, if happiness is to be ours, the proportion of negative to positive must be as the salt is to the loaf. It seemed to me the whole of evolution was a matter of correcting these proportions.

The day's experience had shown me that with each stage

of human development the positive qualities had become more numerous and could be felt with greater frequency and intensity. In contrast to the rage, hatred, and terror of prehistoric man and beast, I again felt the tenderness of the black mother, knew the integrity of Socrates, relived the reverence of the Buddhists, created the art of Michelangelo, and listened to the music of Toscanini. Then, as was characteristic of this paradise, I was in turn overwhelmed by feelings of forgiveness, compassion, love, and other such emotions; and I knew that evolved man would experience these feelings to a far greater degree than we are now capable of.

Somehow I had always thought of evolution as the sum total of changes which had occurred in the past. Now I perceived that the tremendous struggle still continues for every plant, animal, and human; that life must never be thought of as static; and that if any part of life fails to develop with an upward rise, it would eventually be obliterated, as had so much of life in eons past.

Next there flashed into my mind the statement that man differs from animals because he can think, and I knew it to be relatively unimportant; that persons who stress this fact had missed the point. My newly found insight told me the significant difference was that evolved man can love and feel all positive emotions to a far greater degree than can animals. I became aware that it was terror which keeps the negative feelings uppermost and that security is the only hand which can turn emotions to their positive side.

My many emotions of the day had been so all encompassing that they left me with another unshakable conviction which crystallized in this paradise: it is that all plants, animals, and humans alike have much the same feelings you and I have. For the first time in my life, I became aware of a wonderful oneness existing between all living things, whether plant, animal, or human, whether prehistoric, historic, or present. We had each faced the infinitely treacherous struggle for survival; we had each responded to the upward pull of God. I wept because of the wonder of a oneness so great.

Almost simultaneously it occurred to me that the life force felt by every living cell, from the lowest ameba to the most highly developed man, was like gravity which pulled down on all things at all times in all places through all ages, which had always been and always will be. This God gravity, however, was in reverse, exerting its force by drawing ever and always upward, ceaselessly since time began and to be continuous throughout all eternity. Furthermore I knew that as long as we grow to the maximum of our potential, the serenity and peace which then cradled me can be ours; but that the moment our progress becomes one whit less than our best, we experience a restlessness which knows no quieting. With this understanding of evolution, I became aware that man would continue to develop, not so much because of himself but in spite of himself. This conclusion brought me a refreshing, newly found optimism.

A feeling of deep reverence came over me as I perceived that the God force had been responsible for the development not only of man's body and mind but of his soul as well. It seemed to me the soul consisted of many attributes: our positive emotions; our deepest wisdom; our creative abilities; and the sum total of all our potentialities for goodness. I felt that this portion of ourselves which I believed to be the soul was also a part of God, and I knew that God is eternal. What had heretofore been merely an intellectual concept thus became an emotionally charged conviction: that our souls, the God part of ourselves, would live throughout all eternity, remaining forever deathless.

At last I had grasped, in part at least, what God is, and with a tremendous surge of joy, I realized that I had found Him. "God isn't just love, as the Bible says," I kept repeating excitedly. "God is every positive emotion: love, compassion, mercy, kindness, and all the others. Each time I see these emotions being expressed, I am in reality seeing God. He's right here in this garden! I can see Him now in Frank's face and Dr. Snow's and Helen's." Mounting excitement made my heart race; my new discovery seemed so wonderful and so fulfilling, so simple and yet so profound. Furthermore I realized then that God is in each of us to the extent that these positive emotions are in each of us; and He is still in every person, regardless of how hidden these qualities may sometimes be.

Next my thoughts went to my children, and I was overwhelmed with such an intensity of love for them that I suspect it can be recaptured only in this paradise. They seemed like precious jewels it was my privilege to guard—and nothing more—for a short time only. Deep gratitude for the association with them and with my husband filled me.

In another moment of insight, I saw that the whole point of the many torturous feelings I had suffered during the day was a means by which one could understand fully the slow transition from the negative emotions to the positive ones which make up the soul. It was indeed the very evolution of the soul, the God part of one's self, which I had been given the envious privilege of viewing. And I recognized that God, Whom I had so long sought and, with the aid of LSD, had so quickly found, was the whole of this paradise which lay deep within every person.

A feeling of bliss and reverence had settled over me like a soft haze. Then it was swept aside by a wave of genuine humility, and for the first time in my life I felt in awe of myself as an unimportant part of humanity. The fact that I was unimportant was tremendously unimportant. Peace and joy engulfed me, and I knew that the kingdom of heaven was truly within and that LSD had made this day the most important one in my life.

CHAPTER 4

Rejoice! Rejoice! Rejoice!

SEVERAL WEEKS after I had been given LSD, I stood talking to Bill, a psychotherapist who had just finished reading my account of evolution. "Would you like to have the drug again?" he asked casually.

The mere thought filled me with excitement. "Of course!"

"Dr. Janiger's studying its effects on creativity. He's on the lookout for writers. I'll see if he'll take you."

We went into Bill's office. He continued talking as he reached for the phone and dialed. "Just by chance some of the first people he gave LSD to found they had creative capabilities they'd never suspected. The drug appears to bring out latent potentialities. So now Dr. Janiger's exploring its use on the creative ability of writers, artists, musicians, and sculptors."

Bill turned his attention to the phone conversation. He stressed that I was an author of several books and had already been screened by the university group.

Then he turned to me. "Would December 31 be all right?"

"Perfect." I felt as if the key to heaven had been dropped in my lap.

When the exciting date approached, Frank was away, and

I faced a transportation problem. To drive a car the day you are given the drug is unsafe. Since the noise of a hotel on New Year's Eve might interfere with LSD visions, I arranged to spend the night with an old friend, Mrs. Eleanor Smith, who lives near Dr. Janiger's office.

On the morning of the year's end, I awoke early, limited my breakfast to a cup of black coffee, and drove through a sparklingly clear sunrise to Mrs. Smith's. After putting my car in her garage, I visited with her over another cup of coffee while awaiting the taxi to take me to my appointment.

During our conversation, she chanced to mention death. "I don't dread death," she remarked. "It's only a different form of life."

Perhaps it was because I agreed with her that her words stayed with me and influenced my experience.

I arrived at the psychiatrist's office simultaneously with Dr. Henry Hill, a psychotherapist with whom I had worked. Although he had never taken LSD himself, he had generously volunteered to be my monitor.

Before I was given the drug, Dr. Janiger's secretary, Eve, took my history, asking me many questions. Among others were: "Have you ever been given an IQ test? If so, what was the result?"

My answer contained a generous element of smugness. Brains had been highly valued in our family, and I felt mine had served me well. This question too was to influence the experience.

At 9:30 A.M. Dr. Janiger came in and gave me tablets containing 150 micrograms of LSD. He suggested that Eve show Henry and me through the suite and allow us to select the room in which we wished to spend the day. As we followed her, I noticed with a good feeling of security that the equipment and personnel were those of a small hospital.

One room had been converted into a studio and contained a kachina doll which Eve said the artists used as a model. Leaning against the walls were paintings of the doll done before, during, and after LSD was given the artists. In another room I noticed stacks of tape recordings; Eve explained that they had been made by musicians and composers who seemed to find their work much more spontaneous and expressive of deep meaning during and after the drug experience than before it.

Several rooms contained white hospital beds, but we selected a more homelike one with drawn draperies, a comfortable couch for me, and a large easy chair for Henry. I put on the recorder my tape of Leontyne Price singing French and German songs and then, before lying down, drew the chair as near the couch as possible. If the bloodcurdling terror of the first experience should recur, I planned to seek security by grabbing Henry's hand or even throwing myself into his arms. Later I felt that his very presence and the warmth and closeness of our friendship did much to determine the joyousness of the experience.

I covered myself with a blanket and lay listening to the music. Perhaps twenty minutes after taking the drug, I felt first chilled, then frozen. Shivering shook my entire body, and my teeth chattered. Both effects rapidly increased in violence and continued for an hour or longer. Henry threw my coat over me, then brought a second blanket. Only later did I recognize that this intense cold was a form of terror.

Soon I, as myself, ceased to exist, and I became a brilliant chartreuse glowworm with two dozen or more lovely feet which ran the length of my underbody, a suggestion of delicate pink showing at each toe. My large black eyes were like miniature reflecting pools. I was sparsely covered with silken hairs about one-fourth inch long which shone with an intense chartreuse phosphorescence. Along both sides of my back were several small spots of luminous red which glowed like tiny lanterns. I constantly undulated with exquisite rhythm and grace, the free-flowing movements passing the length of my body. Then I could see my glowworm self walking, my dainty feet perfectly synchronized, the middle of my body rising gracefully in the air while some six of my rear feet took their place near an equal number of front ones. These undulations I imitated with what I then considered to be as much charm as if I were a member of the Bolshoi Ballet, my entire body in constant motion.

Although my teeth continued their violent chattering, I was now merely eating grass. Surrounding me was a forest of brilliant new-green grass stems through which filtered an intensely golden supersaturated sunlight. I seemed to be enveloped by the enchanting woodland music of an orchestra of wind-blown leaves and grasses, small insects, and winged creatures. Its rhythm was that of my effortless undulations, and to my sensitive glowworm ears it had both a lilting quality and a Wagnerian touch.

Exaggerated emotions, characteristic of the first LSD experience, already overwhelmed me. I felt a vibrant aliveness, an inexhaustible energy, and a keen appreciation of the beauty of the music, my surroundings, and myself, although totally without egotism. Indeed my admiration of myself was like that of an artist viewing a good painting. Blended with these feelings were peace, harmony, carefreeness, and joy of rhythm and movement, the composite resulting in ecstasy. With Browning, I felt, "God's in his heaven/All's right with the world."

"My IQ's nil," I wanted to exclaim joyously, "but I'm gloriously happy without a care in the world." And on I waltzed in a state of euphoric bliss.

The wave passed, and Henry and I chatted for a few minutes. Soon I wanted to see what would happen next and closed my eyes, awaiting further developments. I became aware of the recording, but instead of French and German songs, Leontyne was singing a single English word: "Rejoice! Rejoice! Rejoice!"

Suddenly my body was shaken by a terrific force, as if by a machine used for mixing paint; something told me the shaking indicated the beginnings of a new life. Immediately I became a magnificent feminine Pegasus of the purest white, the size of a large pony, artistically chubby, and with a lovely arched neck. My glistening white mane and tail had a silky quality. I had huge wings of snow-white feathers laid in perfect symmetry, dainty shell-pink nostrils, and large liquid-blue eyes. My opalescent hoofs were of iridescent mother-of-pearl. Awareness of my beauty made me intensely happy, the emotion again completely uncontaminated by egotism. In addition, all the feelings experienced by the glowworm, such as vibrant aliveness and total harmony, were still mine.

Slightly above me and to my left at all times was a magnificent ebony stallion, his coat shining like a mirror. His huge black wings and thick, waving mane and tail were silken like my own but were much longer than mine. His right wing constantly stretched over me, giving me an exquisite feeling of being both caressed and infinitely protected. Together and in absolute unison, we galloped among fleecy clouds of soft pastel colors.

While under the drug, I cared not one whit that the Pegasus of Greek mythology was a stallion. In this characterization, I thought of myself only as Pegasus, yet an extremely feminine one.

Each minute as we galloped through the skies, I loved everyone in the world but particularly the winged stallion.

In turn I was loved by him to such a degree that my entire body throbbed with the wonder of it. I felt ecstatic, saturated with delight, security, joy, and especially a marvelous energy which demanded to be used. The two of us had no need to talk; we communicated telepathically and yielded to each other's every wish instantly.

"My IQ's zero," I wanted to shout. "Yet I'm bursting with happiness!"

At this point I had to share my joy with Henry. "I'm a beautiful feminine Pegasus, and my IQ's zero. When you're as lovely as I am, you have no need for an IQ."

Henry laughed heartily and quite understandably, but I resented his laughter. I was in dead earnest, and this was no laughing matter.

Intolerant of prosaic life, I quickly recalled that we had not visited Mars recently. Off through space we galloped to the delightful rhythm of symphonic music which seemed more exquisite than anything I had ever heard. I thought of the *William Tell* Overture used with the Lone Ranger shows and considered it as nothing compared to this marvelously carefree masterpiece of the skies. In addition to the delights of free-flowing movement, rhythm, and music, we could see with the miracle of LSD vision in every direction through the thousands of light-years of space to what seemed to be the very borders of the nothingness of infinity.

At intervals in this space hung pastel clouds which appeared to be made of jeweled mists, interesting and varied in shapes and sizes. We played leapfrog over many, diving under or swerving around others. The more massive clouds in our path quickly enveloped us in sparkling opalescence. Throughout this trip I could see a few small planets vast distances away. Although at no time did I recognize the sun as such, the whole of space was saturated with a golden light, as if it were made of transparent gold dust. The immensity and total beauty were so great that they made me feel completely obliterated as myself. This selflessness, alone, was a joyous thing. Yet never was I more alive, and we galloped on and on and still on, overcome with a sense of euphoria all the while.

As we neared Mars, the glistening red sphere gradually grew larger. At last we rested on a cloud, snorted repeatedly, and rubbed our necks together in an ecstasy of delight as we obseved it. The planet was surrounded by swirling pastel mists, like transparent veils made of near-microscopic jewels.

In the meantime, I had been practically shaking both myself and the couch to pieces, every muscle in my body seeming to be in constant motion. My continuous and vigorous lunges suggestive of galloping were so genuine that my entire body was painfully sore for more than two weeks afterward. Now my repeated snortings were being done so enthusiastically that I could feel sprays of moisture falling back on my face. I attempted to reach for a facial tissue, but my hand was doubled into a fist simulating a hoof and try as I might, I could not open it. Suffice it to say both that an LSD-induced characterization is entered into wholeheartedly and that it is extremely difficult to pick up anything with a hoof, even one of mother-of-pearl.

Dr. Janiger came in to ask how I was getting along.

"I'm a gorgeous Pegasus galloping through space," I exclaimed excitedly.

"Who am I to interrupt that?" he replied kindly, and quickly left the room.

After a few more snortings and neck rubbings, we resumed our interplanetary galloping. As we turned toward Saturn, I remembered that we must be careful to dodge its nine satellites. The space around our earth and moon was, I felt, no longer safe; the Americans and Russians were hurtling too much hardware about, projects I viewed with complete disapproval. For this reason we avoided our planet. After visiting Saturn we galloped off to Mercury, then to Venus, Jupiter, Neptune, and Pluto, somehow always aware of the exact location of each. All of these planets glowed with different luminous colors, one seemingly more exquisite than the next, and each was enveloped in swirling transparent mists so lovely that their beauty made me drunk with ecstasy. Yet in addition there was a constant awareness of the gold-filled vastness of space, the demanding rhythm of the magnificent music, the joy of surging vitality, and a multiplicity of other intense emotions, overpowering in their unity.

A period of clarity came, and Henry told me that our interplanetary travels had taken more than three hours. Despite the joy which went with them and the fact that Pegasus was tireless, my actual self felt utterly exhausted. As I lay resting, my thoughts turned to the amazing contrasts between this experience and the earlier one. During the first, every plant, animal, and person had seemed to live and breathe. Most of the landscapes had appeared so real that it was almost impossible to believe they were only visions. Now my world was one of fantasy, and not a single color had been like anything produced by man. Every scene had been color plus light plus jewels of such indescribable beauty as to make the colored lights we are familiar with—neon lights, Christmas tree lights, traffic signs, and rear car lights—seem crude indeed. Although the emotions this time were as intense as were those in the marshes, they seemed to lack meaning. Then came an inward knowing that a deep meaning lay hidden in the experience.

The recording again claimed my attention. Leontyne was still singing, "Rejoice! Rejoice! Rejoice!"

Suddenly I heard two voices: one appeared to be myself as any representative of humanity; and the other belonged to the lovely white Pegasus. These voices continued throughout much of the remainder of the experience. Hereafter, when I took the form of another character, Pegasus was invariably near me. As she, I seemed to have been traveling through space since time began and would continue throughout all eternity.

"Look here, Pegasus," the first voice said disapprovingly. "Eternity's a long time. What's there to rejoice about? Surely there's something more to life than joy."

"Is there anything wrong with joy?" she asked quickly.

"Nothing, but for all eternity it's like living on cotton candy. It's light and frothy. Life should have more depth and dignity."

Her voice was tolerant. "Why not see if you can find something better?"

Instantly I seemed to be in the vortex of a hurricane; every cell of my body was shaken to its very roots by a swirling tempest. Then with no sensation of cold, I watched huge snowflakes falling, their movements like those of a gently waving curtain. Next I became a snowflake and at the same time viewed, as if under a microscope, my intricate symmetrical beauty set with glittering diamonds. As this snowflake I felt the intense aliveness, joyousness, boundless energy, and the many other glad emotions I had experienced as both the glowworm and Pegasus. With other snowflakes of various exquisitely delicate designs, each flake sparkling with ever-changing iridescence, I danced in golden sunlight to the alluring rhythm of a symphony of the snows. This music, slightly suggestive of Tchaikowsky's *Waltz of the Flowers* if played softly, seemed so lovely I felt it could not be surpassed in beauty.

"Only a snowflake could have ears sensitive enough to hear this captivating delicacy of sound," I thought, awed by the wealth of both visual and auditory delights.

All too soon the disapproving voice destroyed my heaven. "This is the same thing. More cotton candy."

Next I became two dice being shaken violently in a box and then rolled onto a table, my actual body shaking as if in the grip of a severe epileptic seizure. This time I was a fish, exquisite, shy, and daintily feminine. My body was tiny, of phosphorescent orange dotted with silver, but my fins were huge and inconceivably thin and graceful; soft lights played from within them as I moved through the water. Around me other small fish of indescribably bright colors, each lighted from within, were darting in rhythm to a water symphony of great delicacy, the pleasant sounds of bubbling, gurgling, lapping, and splashing woven into its melody. Together we explored caverns carved into huge cinnamon-colored stones whose rounded openings were worn to glassy smoothness. The caves were lit, as was the sea around us, with soft golden lights similar to the star-dust tint of space, and the constant movement of the water caused shafts of yellow radiance to appear and disappear.

As we swam, the emotions felt by the glowworm, Pegasus, and the snowflake were again bursting at every cell of my body. While gentle ocean currents rocked me in this state of euphoria, I felt that the privilege of being alive, alone and in itself, gave life adequate meaning.

The room had come back into focus, and for a few minutes I felt like my normal self again. I regretted that the day was being dull for Henry and was passing far too rapidly for me. He suggested coffee, then left but quickly returned with tea which tasted vile, coffee which seemed cold despite rising steam, and chicken broth so delicious that I drank two cups of it.

As I sipped the broth, my thoughts turned to the almost unbelievable fact that beautiful original music was somehow stored deep inside me. With overwhelming astonishment, it occurred to me that if I ever learned enough about technique, I could be a composer. I felt convinced that anyone who could compose mediocre music would, if given LSD, become truly great; and that deep inside every person must be a fount of music which men like Brahms, Beethoven, Mozart, and Schubert had been able to reach. Only later did I learn that other persons given LSD had reported hearing exquisite music not played by human hands.

Soon I was back under the drug. This time I became part of a golden autumn afternoon, the sky so clear that I was lifted into it, seemingly by beauty itself. Balmy Indian-summer breezes blew me far above trees in gaudy dress. All about me were fairies of milkweed seeds, their fragile silken wings delicately lit from within. The fairies, their slender arms and legs moving with infinite grace, seemed to toe-dance on miniature feet covered with pointed slippers glistening with jewels. I had been so fascinated by watching them that I had not at first realized that I too was a fairy. The discovery of my tiny body, my lovely opalescent wings, and my graceful movements caused an excess of joy to penetrate every cell of my actual self. With a combination of dancing, flying, and floating, each movement ecstasy translated into rhythm, we went ceaselessly upward to dainty pastel clouds which we used as seats. Then in our hands there materialized tiny golden flutes, lyres, harps, and mandolin-like instruments inlaid with precious stones. Together we made music such as, I suspect, even angels have never heard. The total beauty was so profound that it changed into pain, and I sobbed, bursting with happiness and yet feeling I could stand no more.

The complaining voice, which I was beginning to hate, came again. After every muscle in my body had been seized as if by a violent convulsion, the dice once more rolled across the table. This time I was a tiny sea horse, rather coy and pleased with myself, swimming with other sea horses in light-filled golden water. As we frolicked about, I thought, "What fun we're having! I didn't know there could be such joy and freedom in rhythm and movement." At the same time I had an urge to urinate and looked frantically for a spot in the ocean to use as a toilet, thinking, "This is real irony. A sea horse who can't find a place to pee."

Even the sensations in my bladder came with the same rhythm of Pegasus' galloping and of all other movements I had experienced. As Henry helped me to and from the rest room, we passed through the studio where an intensely serious young artist, mops of black hair falling over his face, was painting the kachina doll.

As soon as I was comfortable on the couch once more, I became in quick succession a golden harp and then a violin, each instrument being played by unseen hands; many wood winds blown by unknown lips; and a great ray of sunlight which broke into the colors of the spectrum. The gay, happy music of the instruments became shifting, brilliant lights and colors, and the spectrum became music of great purity and delight. As both music and light, I danced joyously to rhythms identical to those of the forms of life I had already experienced. Later I was told that the changing of music to colors and of colors to music are mentioned in many LSD reports.

The searching voice interrupted and seemed pleading now.

"Doesn't life have a deeper purpose than this?"

As the dice came to a standstill on the table, I found myself to be an indescribably delicate jellyfish, seemingly too fragile to contain as it did the intense feelings of exuberance, joyous aliveness, and the other gripping emotions I had already experienced many times. My mere sheet of transparent cytoplasm appeared to be lit from within by soft colored lights which changed in intensity to the rhythm of still another lovely water symphony. The outlines of my body glowed with tiny burning rubies, sapphires, emeralds, and topazes. As I undulated gracefully in water, which was like liquid sunshine, arms of cytoplasm gently oozed out and withdrew in rhythm while other arms formed, their jewels sparkling with their movements. Then I floated weightlessly in the surf and was repeatedly covered by a wealth of warm, breaking bubbles iridescent with multicolored lights. The total luxury made me so awed, breathless, and giddy that I wanted no more, and seemingly of my own volition came out from under the drug.

Henry was nodding sleepily. I suspected that he regretted having volunteered as monitor, although his presence filled me with gratitude. Neither of us spoke. Instead, I was thinking of Frank's comments after he had taken LSD. His experience had been a deeply religious one in which he was so moved by intense beauty and the magnitude of God's love and compassion that he had wished "someone would turn off the valve." He felt that, if he could die right then, he could keep the tremendous beauty and rich emotions for himself throughout eternity. He contended that LSD should be given to all persons suffering terminal illnesses; not only would their agonies be hushed, but their passing could be an event of great happiness.

Now I felt, as he had, that if I could only die, my joyousness could be maintained throughout unending time. And I prayed that some kindly physician, standing beside my death-bed, would inject into my collapsing veins a final dose of loveliness which I could take into the unknown land.

CHAPTER 5

The Golden Light

IT WAS already late afternoon, and I felt that the real meaning of the second experience had not yet come into focus. Did I imagine there was such a meaning?

For some time hunger pangs had been gnawing at me as persistently as a rat gnaws a partition dividing him from a corncrib. At my request, Henry brought more chicken broth and, as he returned, Dr. Janiger's associate, Dr. Davidson, came in with him. I had met Dr. Davidson at a party some two weeks earlier and had found him so warm, cordial, and intelligent that we had become old friends at our first meeting. After a brief visit, during which he offered to drive me to Mrs. Smith's when he had finished seeing patients, he left the room.

Soon my thoughts turned to painting and how all the scenes had made me want desperately to paint them. I longed for a freeing of talent and for both brilliant, luminous colors and the most delicate of pastels. Landscapes I had painted from memory or photographs had given me considerable pleasure, but after I had taken LSD, they became earth-bound bits of attractive real estate, and I had not wanted to touch a brush for two months. Now I felt that hereafter my source material could come only from deep within myself, not something from without; and that I would continue painting as long as I lived.

The galloping had caused my dress to become so uncomfortably bundled around my waist that I now removed it, remaining covered with a blanket. Before me there appeared a vision of a large group of people whom I believed to be nude; yet they were not nude. They wore long red mufflers which they slowly unwound until yards of narrow material hung from their necks. With jerky, ugly movements, they removed coats, dresses, jackets, skirts, ties, and collars. Yet always under each layer of outer clothing there remained still other layers of outer clothing. I realized that their garments symbolized the veneer, the restricting conventions, and the marked unnaturalness characteristic of our society, all of which remain after actual clothing is removed. The startling contrast between these people and the joyous unawareness of self I had experienced as glowworm, Pegasus, and fish threw me into a deep depression.

As the first group disappeared, there came into view still another group whom I knew to be truly without clothing; but they too were not nude. The men wore loose robes, and the women had on beautiful saris of materials which seemed to be spun of spider webbing and of colors such as this world has yet to produce. One man was dressed in the most royal of Tyrian purples; and a charming woman beside him wore a gown of glistening orange-red. These people seemed so full of gladness that their very robes were joy woven into fabric, their every movement a form of esthetic dance. As they changed rhythm into grace, precious stones glistened from the folds of their clothing.

"What is it these truly nude possess which gives them such joy?" I demanded.

Instead of an answer, I immediately became the lovely white Pegasus, cantering this time above our earth. Below me I could see New Year's Eve parties in thousands of homes, restaurants, and ball rooms. I heard their horns, whistles, and raucous laughter and saw their balloons, paper caps, and flowing liquor. Over Times Square I watched thousands of people milling about, singing, yelling, and tooting horns. Instantly the scene shifted: a baby was lying in a crib merrily shaking a rattle. I felt tremendously sad, knowing that joy which must be hunted or forced is a mockery, a baby's rattle compared to the ecstasy it had been my privilege to feel throughout most of the day.

The door opened, and a young man of perhaps nineteen came in; he was deeply under LSD and had escaped from his monitor for a moment. I felt convinced that he was pitifully psychotic. To me, his head appeared to be an empty shell, like an empty peanut hull; and his eyes were hollow spheres made of luminous, gristle-like substance. His body seemed not to exist.

Feeling compassion for him, I cried out, "Why, why does he have to be insane? Why does anyone have to be insane?"

"You know the answer," Pegasus replied.

I made a tremendous effort to think of the reasons for insanity. Finally I asked, "Is it because such people have not found God?"

Pegasus seemed to be trotting beside me. "Of course. Of course."

I felt lost in despair. "I *must* find God," I declared sadly.

Next there appeared before me a large Plymouth Rock hen, her head bent almost to the ground and her neck curved in such a way that she could look at the underside of a leaf. After a glance, she ran to look under another leaf and still another and another. There quickly followed a vision of a mole rooting frantically underground. He would stop a moment, start in another direction, root rapidly for awhile, and then change course again, rooting furiously each time.

"What is it you're looking for?" I asked both the hen and the mole.

Each of them gave the same reply: "I am looking for God."

I burst into tears, feeling that I, like the hen and the mole, had spent my life looking for God in the wrong places and in the darkness. "Where can I look for Him?" I asked myself.

My search was frantic now. The violent convulsions were repeated, and dice again rolled on the table. This time I seemed to be the son of some ancient emperor of China; though I had lived for hundreds of years, I was still young. Rich maroon robes decorated with gold braid fell loosely from my shoulders. As a marvelous horseman, I was riding a spirited stallion over narrow mountain trails. Towering peaks rose high above me. Well content with life, I felt the wind against my cheeks and knew the delight of rhythm as my body and my horse moved in perfect unison. I loped past huge pagodas whose several tiers of roofs were covered with gold leaf, and past great monasteries where thousands of monks had lived, prayed, and died.

I seemed to have been seeking the meaning of life for hundreds of years and to have arrived at a hedonistic philosophy: pleasure is all that matters. I, as the young prince, was thinking as I rode, "The people who worshiped in these temples and who lived in these monasteries thought they knew the answers. But they didn't. Even Christ, Buddha, and Mohammed could each be sued for plagiarism."

The prince's irreverence shocked me; yet I wanted to ask him what he meant by accusing these great men of plagiarism. Before I could speak, he had disappeared. I disagreed with his philosophy so heartily that I knew instantly the rich emotions I had experienced held some deeper meaning than the mere importance of pleasure.

Pegasus was again at my side.

"He's wrong," I declared emphatically. "Christ, Buddha, and Mohammed each did tremendous good."

"That's true," Pegasus answered softly, "but the teachings of these holy men were not original. They would be the first to tell you that. Some few people, like these three, can tap universal wisdom—God wisdom, if you like—and pass it on to others. But deep inside, each person possesses this wisdom, and disbelief cannot keep it from being so."

I was back in reality once more and lay thinking how true it was that each person held wisdom deep within himself. I recalled the statement, "From the conscious mind comes intellect; from the unconscious, wisdom." Then I turned to Henry and urged him to go home, giving him my heartfelt thanks for staying with me. I knew the room was watched on one side by Eve and on the other by Dr. Davidson. Besides, I wished to be alone, thinking that my feelings would then be more intense. As soon as Henry left, I was under the drug again.

"I must continue my search for God," I stated wearily.

Instantly I was Pegasus galloping through space, this time circling our globe and looking down on two thousand years of great universities. Over India I watched a multitude of students who were attending the Buddhist universities long before the time of Christ. We stopped above ancient Babylon, Athens, and Rome; flew on to Heidelberg, Cambridge, and Oxford, and then to the universities in our country, one after another. "Here are learned scholars and philosophers, wise and respected professors," I thought. "These men have spent their lives finding the meaning of life. They can tell me where to find God."

I felt excited and near the end of my search.

Before me came a Persian philosopher, incredibly ancient, who seemed to have lived for centuries and yet still lived. His skin was like old parchment; his chin was covered by a long white beard; his shoulders were bent, and his frail body leaned heavily against a crooked stick. He seemed to be a composite of all scholars, professors, and philosophers of every age. Before my eyes he turned to stone.

I was horrified. "Why have all these great men turned to stone?" I demanded with both alarm and resentment.

"Because they thought intellect was the only thing that mattered," Pegasus answered quietly. "They refused to let their feelings live. Yet God can be found only through the heart."

Overpowering sadness filled me as I went wearily on with my search. It seemed then that I continued searching throughout many fruitless years. At long last I saw in laboratories in many parts of the world hundreds of nuclear scientists. "Perhaps they can show me the answer," I exclaimed hopefully. "They're brilliant and young and fine."

The lines of the ridiculous verse flashed through my mind:

Oh, we can be thankful and grateful and proud
That man's been endowed with a mushroom-shaped cloud;
And we can be certain on some happy day
That someone will set the spark off,
And we'll all be blown away.

There was a deafening "Bang! Bang! Bang!" Instantly I appeared to be in the center of a gigantic Fourth of July sparkler thousands of feet in diameter. With perfect symmetry and against a background of darkness, rays, darts, and spears of light shot seemingly for miles in every direction, each breaking into hundreds of brilliant shooting stars, masses of sparks being thrown out from every star. This inexpressibly spectacular scene was not only beautiful to an infinite degree, but I viewed it with an amazing all-directional vision, as if my entire body had fallen away, leaving nothing except an all-seeing eye. The magnificence of the display left me overcome with awe. Before I could collect my wits, there came a gentle "piff, piff, piff," and gray clouds formed, followed by graceful showers of brilliant star dust.

In a flash my mood changed from one of being stunned by awe and beauty to one of horror and helplessness. "They've blown up our planet!" I cried. "How unutterably dreadful!"

"There's nothing dreadful about it," Pegasus replied calmly. "That silly little planet needed to be blown up. All they've ever thought about was war, war, war. They've been fighting wars for hundreds of years. They tried to use their brains too much and failed to use their hearts. They forgot how to seek God."

"But millions of people have been killed, been blown to bits."

Then Pegasus used the identical words Mrs. Smith had spoken earlier in the day. "They've only changed form, that's all. No one's been killed." The tenderness of compassion came into her voice. "Some had worn-out bodies. Many were in pain. Thousands were crippled; others blind. Even the youngest and healthiest had tremendous problems. Now they're all at peace."

Then I wept, not in sorrow, but in gladness that our earth was no more.

It was difficult to shake off the mood when I found myself again in the prison of reality. Then I noticed it was dark outside, and, with sheer will power, rose, dressed, and went into the office. Eve introduced me to a photographer who was chatting with her. I took an immediate dislike to him, feeling that he was hopelessly earth-bound and that he was afraid of his emotions and used only his head. Suddenly a force like a battering-ram hit me in the stomach. My arms and legs became rigid, and I felt myself, like the scholars and philosophers, turning to stone. I staggered stiff-leggedly back to the couch and gratefully lay down again, soon realizing that the photographer had served as a mirror in which I had seen an unsavory truth about myself. At last it came to me that one could never find God by intellectual probing, and that spiritual wealth could be gained only by allowing rich emotions to live within one's heart.

The light had hurt my eyes, but with the door closed the room was completely dark. Suddenly I was gazing in awed wonder and again with the miracle of spherical vision at millions of brilliant stars which surrounded me in every direction, dotting the skies into endless space. The whole of the universe seemed to be filled with celestial music, the humming of the solar systems as they rotated in their orbits. Then I was a star in the very midst of the heavens, then another star, and still another, each ceaselessly moving through endless space and eternity. Next I became an entire solar system, then a second, and a third, rotating on and on through eons of time. Simultaneously I held up my left hand, fist lightly closed, and swung my right hand in increasingly larger circles around it, representing the rhythm of moons around planets and planets around suns and solar systems around other solar systems, *ad infinitum*. As the magnificent music of the spheres rose in overpowering crescendo, I felt within me the same glorious rhythm I had experienced all day, whether as Pegasus, fish, or fairy, as music, light, or snowflake. Now I knew this joyous rhythm to be no less than the rhythm of the universe itself, a universe so perfect in plan and function that it could be created only by the hand of God; a universe so perfect that even the destruction of our earth could not disturb it. At that instant there was born in me a new faith in God and a new optimism which put down roots of permanence. I knew that at last I was beginning to find God, and I sobbed with gratitude so overwhelming that it became pain.

When Dr. Davidson came to take me to Mrs. Smith's, I was still crying and in no mood to talk. The knowledge that he had been given LSD many times made me feel comfortable to remain silent. As we drove, the Christmas decorations along the streets glittered with exaggerated beauty, and the lighted trees in the windows of homes had a fairyland quality. Yet I longed to be in bed.

Mrs. Smith had scarcely shown me to my room when I started sobbing loudly and uncontrollably. The lights, the slightest noise, even the kindness of my hostess grated on raw nerves. More than anything else, I wanted to be alone, to get back to the world where heaven was real. At the same time, I felt starved and welcomed both the tray when it was brought and the solitude when it was removed.

My sobbing, which at first seemed to be caused merely by fatigue and hunger, continued for an hour or more. I soon realized the tears were of sorrow because the many wonderful emotions I had experienced were so rare in the lives of all people, and of gratitude that such ecstasy had been mine.

From 7:30 that evening, when I was left alone for the night, until I fell asleep well after midnight, I appeared to be as deeply under the drug as at any time during the day. A few intervals between waves, however, became perceptibly longer. Visions I had seen earlier appeared again and again in their original vividness. During this period, many casual thoughts changed to convictions, and my search for God found its fulfillment.

As I nestled into my pillow for the night, I quickly became the lovely Pegasus, curled up on an infinitely soft cloud, my handsome stallion companion lying on another cloud beside me. For a time a tremendously peaceful and soothing joy pervaded every cell in my body. Then the buoyant aliveness returned, and we resumed our travels through space.

My vigorous movements which simulated galloping caused the head of the bed to bang against the wall, the springs to squeak inharmoniously. "Pegasus, why don't you fly rather than gallop?" I demanded. "It would be so much smoother and easier."

"Because I have within me the energy of the universe which must be used," was the answer. "It pervades all things. You experienced it as rhythm."

These words, together with the almost continuous rhythms I had felt during the day, left in me an unshakable conviction that there is indeed a universal and God-created energy which expresses itself as rhythm in all things, from the path of electrons around protons to solar systems around other solar systems.

Before me appeared again the truly "nude," their arms uplifted in a dance of joy, their magnificent robes falling into graceful swirls with jewels sparkling. It seemed to me these were people who had found God. As if everything one could desire were to be given in a single day, I became the delightful creature in the exquisite orange-red sari, and Frank was he who wore the most royal of Tyrian purples. This time we danced in the golden light of space, seemingly on into eternity in a state of bliss understood only by those who have experienced euphoria. As I wept with joy, feelings of love became so intense that I knew they could only be of divine origin. Then I realized that this feeling was actually God, Who is defined as love and Who is love, residing within myself, and that in the same manner He is in all other persons.

I kept thinking of Frank, so many miles away. "He's not separated from me at all," I exclaimed suddenly. "He's been with me every minute today. He's the beautiful black stallion!" And I continued to cry, feeling that two people who really love can never be separated, not by space or time or eternity. Even the lines in the marriage ceremony, "Till death us do part," seemed utterly ridiculous. Thus another conviction took its place with the others.

Then for a long time visions of the earlier part of the experience again came before me. As my feelings were tossed like crashing ocean waves from the sunlight spectrum bursting into glorious melody to music exploding into an aurora borealis of light-saturated colors, on to snowflakes dancing with wings of joy, fish absorbed in aqueous beauty, and Pegasus consumed with overwhelming love, I felt one could not get closer to heaven.

Gradually the wave passed, and I lay trying to find the meaning of these violent emotions. Suddenly it was as though a film fell from my eyes, and I realized that the fantasies of the first part of the experience were like material in a dream which is cast in such symbols as to make it appear light and unimportant, yet whose meaning is actually profound. As I recalled my earlier conviction that God was not just love but all positive emotions, it occurred to me that every emotion accompanying the fantasies had been a positive one, a God feeling. Experiencing these emotions in all their intensity was both a way for me to discover that I was capable of God feelings and for forcing me to realize that they lay deep within me. The first part of the experience, therefore, had actually been a laboratory course by which I could learn to accept the fact that God was really in me and in every other person.

In another sense, I could see that each of the impersonations, such as Pegasus, fairies, snowflakes, and the like, was a symbol of the part of one's self which longs to take wing, soar into the ether, and commune with the divine. It seemed to me that the feelings of joy, rhythm, appreciation of beauty and music, and the many other emotions I had experienced were all part of an intrinsic spiritual power which pervades the universe, each of them different aspects of God.

Then for the last time I became the joyous white Pegasus accompanied by my beloved stallion. Together we galloped through the exquisite golden light of space while celestial music of inexpressible beauty seemed to make the rhythm of the universe, of its melody, and of our movements one. We crossed one and then another and another of the millions of Milky Ways which fill infinity. At last I comprehended fully that the joy which possessed me was God; the celestial music which seemed part of me was God; and the exquisite golden light of space was God. In a flash I recalled that I had seen this golden light throughout the day; it had permeated the grasses where the glowworm fed; the ocean where the fish and sea horse played; the air where the snowflake and fairies danced; and the whole of infinity where the planets turned in their orbits. Now, no matter how far we traveled or how many millions of light-years we traversed, there was no darkness. Never diminishing one iota, an endless sea of glorious golden light which was in truth God stretched into infinity. As I watched, an overpowering feeling of reverence settled into my very depths.

It was then I understood that God's light, like the sun, never sets; that just as our earth turns away from the sun, it is we who turn away from God. In the same way this golden light flooded all things, I knew that God penetrated every crevice of the universe, filling every space, regardless of how small, and piercing every wall, regardless of how thick; and that He both filled and surrounded every human being. Thus another conviction became a reality: to find God, we had only to look within ourselves and everywhere around us.

After the wave had passed, I got up and stood gazing out a window; yet I remained so deep in thought that I scarcely noticed the city lights below me to my right or the stars touching the dark hills to my left. Again, as during the first experience, I felt a warm oneness with all that live, a marvelous unity and harmony with the very universe itself. The feeling seemed to result from having been identified with many forms of life and also from being aware throughout most of this experience that I was not myself, but a selfless, egoless, joyous representative of all humanity, loving, searching, and soaring into the infinite.

Once I chuckled softly as I recalled how the glowworm and Pegasus had poked fun at me for being pleased with my IQ, remembering that the first part of the experience, for all its overwhelming emotions, had not contained a single rational thought. Again the fantasies were like dreams in which one does not solve problems by rational thinking: yet a dream itself may be the solution to a problem. Similarly, without rational thought, the experience had been the solution to my problem of trying to find God. At last I could see that when intellectual development is overemphasized, the subjective part of one's self, in which religious experiences occur, is usually underevaluated; thus the finding of God is hindered by the worship of the intellect. For the first time I could understand clearly why, since a religious experience is entirely a subjective one, it could never be found in books or sermons or anywhere except deep within one's self.

The room grew chilly, and I snuggled back into bed. Soon

all infinity seemed filled with an endless ocean of golden light. Then I saw Him! A glorious white-gold radiance emanated from a central source somewhat like the Statue of Liberty in shape and perhaps ten times its size. The area of the face was a glowing white light, soft, warm, and lovely; spears and darts of light shooting out from the head formed a halo. The figure appeared to be made of layer after layer of long flames of pale yellow fire shaped like narrow petals of a gigantic flower, the lower and outer layers growing richer in color until the feet and periphery were pale orange. These petal-shaped flames, which radiated symmetrically downward and outward, danced in rhythm and sparkled like jewels, each and all of exquisite beauty. The continuous movement and the slight variations in the coloring of the flames made it appear that God wore a robe of soft gold fabric which fell into graceful folds and swayed as if blown by a gentle breeze. His upper arms were held close to His body, but the lower arms and open hands reached forward in a gesture of welcome. The whole figure seemed the very embodiment of love, indescribably intense in its impact. God appeared to be saying, "I have been here always, and I shall be here always. I wait to welcome and protect you, but come only when you are ready, only if you wish."

His gesture and words seemed to make visible patience, freedom, tenderness, love, and joy. The glory, wonder, and beauty of it tore me asunder, and I cried aloud, feeling humbled and awed and overcome with reverence, wanting to bow to the ground in the manner of a Moslem worshiping Allah.

While the great radiance still filled the sky, I heard the bells, horns, and whistles welcoming in the new year, a new year which I felt would for me be filled with golden light.

CHAPTER 6

Having Eyes, See Not

"IN OUR STUDY on creativity, we've rarely given LSD to a person more than once, and you've already had it twice," Dr. Janiger was saying. Then his words revealed his innate kindness. "But you've had such rich experiences, it seems a shame to deprive you."

Thus my luck held, and three weeks after my interplanetary traveling as Pegasus, I was off on a third trip to visionland.

Despite my eagerness to search deeper into myself, on the morning of January 20, 1960, my hand trembled as Dr. Janiger placed in it six tiny tablets each containing 25 micrograms of LSD. For two days I had been plain scared. The uncomfortable anxiety had increased so steadily that I was half tempted to change my mind, although at the same time I looked forward to the experience with considerable excitement.

Dr. Davidson, who was to be my monitor, immediately took me into his office. It was a large room attractively furnished with a long sectional davenport and two comfortable lounging chairs between which stood a low but oversized table of irregular shape. A beige carpet accentuated the pleasant colors of the furniture and draperies.

I stretched out on the davenport, and as Dr. Davidson covered me with a blanket, I studied a colorful abstraction on the wall opposite me and a nicely sculptured head on a bookcase at my left. The blinds had been closed for privacy, the room being lighted by a lamp at my right and another behind the davenport. Dr. Davidson covered my eyes with a sleep shade, explaining that darkness helped persons have deeper feelings. Then he put records on the player and took a chair slightly behind me.

The conversation turned to LSD experiences in general. He told me he had monitored persons more than a hundred times and that most people searched for the deeper meanings of life while under the drug. Soon he suggested that talking might delay the experience, and we remained silent for what seemed hours. From time to time he asked, "Anything happening?"

"Absolutely nothing," I answered repeatedly with increasing disgust.

After another long silence, he said, "Some people build up such unconscious resistance that even 400 micrograms of LSD give them no experience."

I felt utterly defeated, convinced that I would have no more enthralling experiences and could never again see beyond-our-world beauty. My key to heaven had been thrown away. Since only LSD could cause a disappointment to be so exaggerated, obviously the drug had already started to take effect.

After another seemingly long delay, which I found painfully embarrassing, Dr. Davidson rose. "Perhaps you'd feel freer alone. I'll be just outside the door where I can hear you if you call."

He had scarcely closed the door when I saw a dozen or more bandits on horseback gallop up a steep hill and attack a medieval castle divided from them by a water-filled moat and closed drawbridge. Armored knights quickly sprang to parapets and hurled long lances at them. As a few bandits and knights fell in battle, I could hear the loud weeping of women from within the castle. The scene shifted abruptly, and I watched chariot races along the Appian Way. The drivers wore armored breastplates and short, pleated tunics. The two elaborately carved, gold-trimmed chariots were each drawn by three horses galloping as if devils were after them. Then nothing happened for a period which seemed hours. I waited with extreme impatience.

Dr. Davidson opened the door. "Anything happening yet?"

I replied quickly, without the slightest doubt that I was telling the truth, "Absolutely nothing." It was not until the following day that I realized I had lied to him.

"Would you like to take 50 micrograms more?" he asked.

"Is it safe?"

"Yes. As much as 1500 micrograms have been given with no apparent harm."

I agreed, and he brought water and two more tiny blue tablets, making my total dose 200 micrograms. Although it had seemed an eternity, he assured me that only one and a half hours had passed. I expressed the desire to be alone, and he again left the room.

Soon I watched in even greater detail the bandits and chariot races. This time I was definitely a fly sitting on the rumps of the horses, enjoying the rides and feeling jolly and impish. Then as I made loud buzzing noises and vigorous body movements appropriate to flying and darting, I inspected a vast uninhabited wilderness which seemed to be the whole of southern Europe as it appeared in prehistoric times.

Simultaneously I was swept into a whirlpool of violent emotions, this time made up of feelings of well-being, buoyancy, utter contentment, effortless movement, inexhaustible energy, and the joys of being in harmony with the beat of life and of soaring unfettered through clear sparkling sunlight with the rush of pleasantly warm air caressing my body. These intense feelings and other kindred ones remained throughout most of the experience. Two other emotions, however, invariably stayed uppermost: the first was the keenest possible awareness of beauty in everything my glance fell upon, together with the deepest imaginable appreciation; and the second was an overwhelming sadness caused by a conviction that no one saw this beauty except myself in the form of whatever characterization the visions portrayed. Again the visions themselves seemed the merest of incidents compared to the intensity of the emotions which accompanied them.

Now as a fly I looked over great forests, mountains, rivers, green slopes, vast plains, and surf-edged seas which first lay like a relief map below me and were then viewed as if from a low-flying plane. Every scene was realistic, but the colors were unusually vivid, and all sparkled in brilliant morning sunshine. At frequent intervals I would swoop down, alight, rub my graceful back legs together, and admire the opalescence of my delicate sunlit wings. Totally without egotism but with deep satisfaction, I stated repeatedly, "I'm beautiful. No one else thinks so, but I really am."

Next I became a spider, then a great variety of spiders, each feeling the vibrant aliveness and keen awareness of surroundings that I had experienced as a fly. I admired, one after another, webs of unusual loveliness covered with dew and lit by morning sun which accentuated the delicacy of the designs and caused the miniature drops to sparkle with multi-colored jewels. I realized that this breath-taking beauty of my creating remained unnoticed, and a tremendous sadness settled over me. As these depressed, frustrated little spiders, I wept heartbrokenly in the corners of my webs.

It seemed that man had not yet appeared on earth and that I was living in a glorified age of insects. Subsequently I became a great variety of winged creatures, each with feelings so intense that it seemed impossible for their small bodies to contain such emotions. I was a gnat with a tiny, mirror-shiny black body and gauzy wings, then a swarm of gnats, flying in unison through warm summer air; a bumblebee covered with silky down of luminous browns and gold, buzzing loudly and joyously with other brightly colored bumblebees around an apple tree gay with blossoms; a single mosquito and soon many mosquitoes with miniature wings, bodies, and legs more graceful than those of any ballet dancer, zooming in joyous flight over marshy swamps. As each of these insects, I admired my body and wings and my surroundings with a deeper admiration than I had known was possible.

In turn I changed into a lively grasshopper, making such appropriate hops that I almost knocked over the lamp behind the davenport; a singing katydid with brilliant green, tissue-paper-thin wings; a locust, regretfully leaving my lovely shell; and a variety of tiny insects unknown to me. Loveliest of all, I became a dragonfly with exquisite dots of opalescent jewels showing on my slender body and delicate wings; and as she, I swooped about over crystal-clear streams.

Successively I found myself to be a great variety of butterflies and moths. As a small yellow butterfly, I darted happily from flower to flower along a dusty country road. As a monarch butterfly, I hovered caressingly over a wind-swept garden ablaze with color. As a large peacock butterfly with phosphorescent blues and greens surrounding circles of brown on my wings, I flew with my strikingly colorful mate over pristine rivers and steaming jungles of what is now Brazil, a riot of bright flowers and birds among masses of green foliage. As a hummingbird moth, whose fragile wings fluttered so rapidly they appeared to be tiny clouds of mist, I sucked from honeysuckle blossoms on a balmy, moonlit night, the odor of the flowers even more pungent than in reality.

Throughout this sequence, I felt such a warm oneness with each of these winged creatures that it has been extremely difficult for me to kill insects since, an attitude I would have formerly considered ridiculous. Now, as each insect, I was overcome by a joyous freedom of flying, the beauty of my body and wings, the grace of my effortless movements, and the charm of my strikingly lovely surroundings. At the same time there continued the deep sadness; the beauty I saw so clearly was not even noticed by anyone else, much less appreciated.

The visions passed, and I lay longing for a powerful magnifying glass and a microscope with which I could examine the bodies and wings of insects, knowing I would find beauty far more exquisite than I had dreamed possible. Furthermore I felt sure that magnified wing textures with LSD colors superimposed on them would make fascinating subjects for painting abstractions; and I yearned to put such ideas into immediate execution.

Simultaneously I kept thinking of a fragment of a Biblical quotation: "Unto one of the least of these." Even the tiniest insect had been beautiful, as had indeed been everything I had seen. A feeling of reverence settled over me as I realized this beauty was God, and He had shown Himself even to and by the least of these.

Soon I was caught in another tidal wave of feelings. I continued to play the double role of viewer and viewed, convinced that I was still back in prehistoric times. In quick succession, I became great expanses of dense forests on plains and mountain slopes of every country of every continent. While I watched them as with a bird's eye, my body swayed with the trees and my voice sang with the wind. I was mighty rivers of every land, later to be named the Amazon, Mississippi, Danube, Ganges, Ob, and Volga, each crystal clear, silver, blue, or green, but all luminous. Like a game of charades, I tried to imitate with body movements the flowing of water, the dancing of rapids, and the washing away of embankments which caused a constant changing of my course.

Next I became great streaks of lightning, cutting sheer splendor into the skies above every sea and continent, my body jerking violently with each mighty bolt. Holding myself in rigid dignity, I was magnificent snow-capped mountain ranges, the whole of the Andes, Himalayas, Rockies, and others. I looked down on my slopes at mighty glaciers melting into lakes of luminous, milky green and up at mist-caressed crags which seemed to be arms, pleading to God. As my voice rose and fell and my body made plunging motions, I became the roaring Niagara and the higher but lesser known falls of Africa and South America, each flamboyant with pastel radiances. Then, relaxing completely and with a joyous feeling of hurtling through space, I fell as the delicate waterfalls of Yosemite where mother earth seemed to hold out her very fingertips to catch me, her brown hands cupping slightly.

Not at all as myself but seemingly as each inanimate

feature, I felt overcome by my awe-inspiring magnificence. Yet always there was the accompanying sadness that such breath-taking beauty went unnoticed. Even at last when primitive man did come, he could not see my greatness. Whether I was mountain or forest or lightning, he was too ready to believe that I held evil spirits and bad omens. Patiently I waited through the passing of millions of years, sobbing aloud at this utter waste of beauty and the lack of appreciation for the generosity of an all-giving God.

The wave passed, and I raised the sleep shade and looked about the room which had seemed unusually attractive. Now it appeared so colorless and dead that I quickly pulled the sleep shade back in place and lay thinking of a poem I had learned long ago. It drummed in my brain, and I could not be rid of it:

A curve in the road and a hillside
Clean cut against the sky;
A tall tree tossed by autumn wind,
And a white cloud riding high;
Ten men went along that road,
And all but one passed by.
He saw the hill and the tree and the cloud
With an artist's mind and eye;
And he put them down on canvas
For the other nine men to buy.

I kept wanting to change the nine persons who failed to see the charm of the landscape to thousands or millions and felt distressed that the verse no longer rhymed.

Next my mind turned to the amazing difference in the visions of this experience compared with the earlier two. These visions lay midway between the stark reality of the first and the sheer bejeweled fantasy of the second. Although everything seemed extremely real and as might be seen in ordinary life, it was nature at her extreme excellence. All the scenes had a pristine quality as if flooded with crystal-clear morning sunlight. Without exception every object was aglitter and asparkle, like diamonds dancing on blue water or new-fallen snow or clean-washed leaves after a rainstorm. Under such light, all colors took on a quality of gems without causing a loss of realism.

Again the drug held sway, and it seemed to me that there was beauty in all of nature, animate and inanimate alike, and that my eyes, meaning the eyes of the entire human race, must somehow be opened to this magnificence and thus to God. There was a tremendous urgency in this feeling, and I felt miserably confused and puzzled as to how such an appreciation could be brought about, convinced that the entire responsibility lay on my shoulders. Then my teeth started to chatter and my lips to move rapidly, movements which continued not only during the remainder of the day but throughout the two following days, stopping only when I was suddenly interrupted and when I slept.

At first I had no idea what these movements of lips and jaws might mean. Then awareness came, and I was a single white segmented silkworm feeding greedily on the underside of a mulberry leaf. The lovely, dull green near my eyes constantly changed intensity and pattern as the sun shifted and the wind blew the leaves on which I fed into the shadows of other leaves. Soon I appeared to be thousands and then millions of silkworms, all feeding on breeze-caressed leaves and undulating as they moved about, my own body attempting to undulate as gracefully as did theirs. While I, as silkworms collectively, continued to eat, a dainty and ever-changing filigree of leaf veins was silhouetted against billowy clouds or sunlit skies of varying blues or bright moonlight. At times I could hear the soft patter of raindrops above me or feel the movement of wind whipping the leaves as I held on tenaciously with my tiny white feet. Usually soft warm breezes caressed my skin, and I felt content and in harmony with life. Only one thing marred my happiness. Though I was once again overcome with the beauty surrounding me, no one else saw it or cared. My sadness was now a massive weight pulling me down into unknown and bottomless depths.

The experience changed character at this point as if the additional 50 micrograms of the drug had suddenly reached my brain all at one time. Although thoughts come with amazing rapidity and clarity when one is under LSD, the intensity of all emotions now increased to overpowering proportions. During the remainder of the day and until 1 A.M. the following morning, ideas bombarded my brain with tremendously increased velocity, hundreds of them seeming to come at once. I felt constantly giddy, hopelessly confused, and literally terrified for fear I was losing my mind. Repeatedly, when it seemed that my head would surely burst, I regretted having taken as much as 200 micrograms of the drug. These unpleasant emotions are lost in the telling, but the memory of them still causes me to cringe. The drug, over which I had absolutely no control, carried me into whirlpool vortexes of ever-increasing magnitude, a terrifying experience even when richly rewarded. I could feel such a wave clutching me now, my identity quickly lost as it swept me from the shores of reality.

This time I, as the sum total of silkworms, determined to dedicate all my energies, indeed the whole of my various lives, to creating so much beauty that people would be forced to notice it. Just as fish must lay thousands of eggs so that one adult of their species might survive, or an oak must produce thousands of acorns so that a single tree might grow to maturity, I felt that I must create thousands of times more beauty than would ever be noticed. By so doing, I believed that at least a thousandth of this beauty would be appreciated.

Although I still continued to eat greedily as a composite of all silkworms, simultaneously I became thousands of gray-white moths laying millions of eggs. With strenuous contractions of my abdomen, which were real indeed, a great bulk of eggs seemed to pass from my body, and immediately a feeling of emptiness followed. As larvae, I hatched easily, ate unceasingly, grew rapidly, and spun cocoons. Instead of producing silk from glands in my lips, as do real silkworms, I appeared to have spinnerets like those of spiders. For hours I rotated my buttocks while there emerged strands of shining limpid material hundreds of yards long which quickly changed to pearly gray-white silk. While rotating continuously, I often drew up my knees, shortening my body as much as possible to catch the threads with my head. Next I would stretch to pull the threads forward. In this manner each thread was properly coiled around my body until the cocoon was finished.

I relaxed momentarily into blissful softness before starting the serious business of growing wings and legs. Emerging from the cocoons was invariably a struggle. Every muscle seemed to fight for release, causing a lamp to rattle so much that Dr. Davidson came in and removed it. My wet wings and legs were helpless at first, and my actual arms and legs felt weak to the point of pain. Quickly I grew in strength and soared joyously into the sky, bred, and repeated the cycle. Regardless of the visions appearing before me, throughout the remainder of the day I was continuously and simultaneously in two or more stages of this cycle.

Then, as in the previous LSD experience, I heard a voice. This time a wise queen of the silkworms served as spokesman. With soothing gentleness she told me, "Every minute of day and night for millenniums we have been creating beauty. Of all living creatures, we have been especially blest: our beauty was seen thousands of years before Christ. Since that time, it has been appreciated in all parts of the world. We are, therefore, more qualified to show you beauty than is any other creature."

In quick succession there passed before me an exquisitely dainty Chinese princess wearing embroidered satin slippers on tiny, bound feet and a robe of brilliant, iridescent blue silk; and an extremely charming Japanese woman who fluttered a white silk fan and was dressed in a purple silk mandarin coat. It seemed to me that these women had lived 5000 years ago. Next I saw on the Indian Ocean a sailing vessel carrying silk to the Tudor queen of England, Elizabeth. A fierce storm arose; angry waves revealed their oceanic wrath, and bearded seamen scurried about, shouting oaths as they tried to save the ship. I watched the vessel sink slowly through clear water of fantastically bright colors, deeper and deeper until it rested on the sandy floor of the ocean. As it settled on its side, blue-green silk tumbled out and unfurled to become one with the rich iridescence of the sea. Then an unbelievably graceful octopus, his body a shiny black lit with purple, blue, and green high lights and his suction cups rimmed with jewels, snuggled into the decaying ship. Lastly I watched at Versailles during the reign of Louis XIV an exquisitely fantastic ball where white-wigged men and women alike wore glistening silks. The ladies' gowns were of lovely pastel colors which shimmered as they danced, as if the silk were a thing alive.

Gradually I came back to reality, but like a person not yet

awake from a deep sleep. Even during moments of clarity, one is far from being free from the influence of the drug. I stood up unsteadily to go to the rest room, feeling it was impossible to walk but preferring to negotiate it alone rather than to call Dr. Davidson. I crossed the room where an attractive, middle-aged woman, deep under LSD, was painting the kachina doll. Like the blind leading the blind, she took my arm and helped me until I was back on the davenport, telling me all the while what a marvelous experience she was having. It seemed to me she was the very embodiment of kindness; and the gentleness of Christ shone from her strong face. How often I have wished that the great love for humanity one feels so strongly when under LSD could be maintained throughout all human relationships.

For the first time since the drug had taken effect, I noticed the music, although I had been vaguely aware that Dr. Davidson had come into the room and put on more records. It was a symphony of Brahms, and despite the fact he had long been one of my favorite composers, the music seemed heavy, earth-bound, and so discordantly ugly I called Dr. Davidson to shut it off. After he had done so, he took a chair behind me. The next wave carried me out with such force I immediately forgot he was there.

Again as silkworms collectively, I continued my age-long task of creating beauty. At the same time the observing part of myself seemed to be both a nameless representative of humanity and a combination of all persons. As combined humanity, I watched the silkworms create beauty for the remainder of the experience and was ever aware that beauty was God. By the sum total of our appreciation, I sensed that the silkworms achieved their goal and that our reverence was their reward. Thus it seemed that the eyes of everyone who lives were opened to beauty and to God.

To get some idea of the indescribable immensity of my vast field of vision during all the following sequences, imagine that on a sparkling clear day you were sitting at the prow of a ship far out on an empty ocean. If you turned your head as far as you could from extreme left to extreme right, you would observe seemingly endless distances to all horizons. During this experience, the entire dome of the sky and all far horizons were visible at each breath-taking glance. The total area filled with fantastic colors was approximately six times that covered by the most spectacular sunset. In addition to the vastness, the skies seemed saturated with sunlight and the air washed to sparkling cleanliness. The total impact was so great that each vision made me feel almost as though a bolt of lightning had struck me, and besides my other body activities, I lay gasping again and again.

As a combination of all silkworms, I had as my first daily task, which had gone on for millions of years, to produce, spin, and weave the silk for the sunrises throughout the world. So much work lay ahead that I seemed to be under terrific pressure. Every hour of every day, the sun was rising over many parts of our earth, and no two flaming skies were ever the same. Furthermore there must be different designs for every season and every degree of humidity, and location must be considered. Ideas were bombarding my brain with as much confusing rapidity as if I were surrounded by dozens of persons firing them from shotguns. To the unceasing activities of eating, spinning cocoons, emerging as moths, laying eggs, and hatching was now added a shuttle-like motion of weaving; thus my body was in a constant frenzy of completely involuntary movements. Although this frantic activity lasted for twelve hours or more, the rewards were so great that I did not feel fatigued at any time.

Before me as a background there stretched a vast empty

sky of nondescript blue-white. Then throughout the remainder of the experience, there appeared at my far left mammoth cocoons from which unrolled, like gigantic bolts of cloth thousands of yards wide, silks of exquisite colors such as surely no one has ever dreamed of. All of these silks glided gracefully across my vast field of vision until the entire sky was covered from dome to horizon and from extreme left to extreme right. They swayed constantly as if blown by a gentle breeze and fell into graceful folds which caught glistening lights and cast rich shadows.

Now as brilliant silk filled the sky, my right arm swept in a 270-degree arc, and like a mighty hanger, I smoothed the glorious sunrise into place. Always I had to make haste; dawn was breaking in many other parts of the world. As the glow of one sunrise faded, another flooded the celestial spaces. In this manner I created sunrise after sunrise, moving ever westward and from north pole to south until sunrises had been made for the entire world. They were all different, all unbelievably lovely, and all seemingly made of burning jewels so fantastically overwhelming in brilliance and vastness that I literally caught my breath as each new bolt of silk unfurled.

By the time the colors of the sunrises had faded, I must have ready blue for all the world's skies. I had no sooner patted several dozen blues of various shades lovingly into the dome of heaven than the colors for setting suns must be woven and ready. Dusks, with their blends of deep blues and blacks and fading lights, had to be prepared and placed with their softer tones near the horizon. With a feeling that the world was too much with me, I realized that night skies were needed to cover half the globe. As the silkworms rapidly wove soft black velvet studded with gold, I worried excessively about the exact point at which the North Star should be eliminated and the Southern Cross appear, dreading any inaccuracy. Since clouds were a part of all skies, they had to be made simultaneously in every shape and shade of grays, blues, whites, off-whites, and sunrise and sunset colors. As glistening veils of soft silks, seemingly woven of spider webbing, swirled across the sky, I gently formed cumulus and alto-cumulus clouds with oversized hands, like making gigantic hamburger patties, and put them carefully in place. The cirrus and stratus clouds I stretched across the heavens as if I were pulling taffy.

All too soon the dark, dreary room came back into focus. Immediately I thought of the many persons I had heard declare that an LSD experience could not be described. "There are no words," they had kept repeating. My feeling had been that they could have described their experiences if they had really tried, but now I wholeheartedly agreed with them.

I exclaimed to Dr. Davidson, "A report of this experience would have to be as long as the six-foot shelf of Harvard classics." And I knew he understood, for he had been faced with the same problem.

There had been much near repetition in the making of the skies, and hours of it would still follow. Though all the scenes were fantastically exciting to watch, they would be monotonous to read about. The remainder of this report, therefore, is purposely summarized and contains perhaps a thousandth of what I actually witnessed. Much more is omitted simply because I can find no words which can do the experience justice.

Soon I was deep under the drug again and realized I had to produce the greens for all the meadows, forests, and growing plants throughout the world. Once more I felt there was so much to be done that my head was bursting. I chewed gum, which served as mulberry leaves, at fantastic speed to keep production equal to the demand. Also I was quickly overwhelmed by the speed with which hundreds of visions appeared before me. This time at my upper left the gigantic cocoons unrolled bolts of various shades of exquisite green silks. Midway in the sky fragments of fabric broke away and fell downward as if blown by a strong wind. Below appeared ever-changing landscapes of exaggerated beauty. Bits of green silk became leaves, ferns, and the foliage of underbrush in a hundred forests. Lighter greens became spring meadows, fields of sprouting grain, and trees in bud.

Then autumn colors were quickly demanded. I had scarcely finished arraying the northern forests in a sheer splendor of crimsons and sunshine yellows when winter had passed and the trees in the southern hemisphere clamored for bright colors.

Next difficult problems confronted me in the creation of materials for snows. Somehow I had to produce snows which glistened in sunshine, woven with millions of diamonds; snows which sparkled in moonlight, sprinkled with star dust; blue snows which could be used for shadows, glaciers, and icebergs; and red, orange, yellow, and lavender snows which reflected the colors of sunrises, sunsets, and the aurora borealis. Lovely silks meeting these specifications soon unfurled and filled the sky with awe-inspiring grandeur. As scenes below shifted from great mountain ranges to moonlit plains to iceberg-clogged oceans to monotonous tundras, each color and shape fell into its proper place.

The next problem was to make the material for mists, inconceivably thin, soft, and silky. As it swung out across the sky, it sparkled as if a delicate pastel light had been spun into every strand. Streams of this fabric fell into graceful shapes below mountain peaks, causing them to seem suspended in air, like charming Japanese prints. I, as a composite of all silkworms, happily used this lovely material to hide man-made ugliness. With my right arm sweeping in wide gestures, I pulled it gently over city slums, unsightly dumps, tenement districts, and gaudy road signs, tucking it into corners as securely as a mother tucks a baby into bed. By this means, ugliness seemed not to be merely hidden but to be magically and permanently removed from the earth.

Soon golden silks, waving in folds of sunlight richness, fell into squares, rectangles, and L shapes and became fields of ripened grain quietly taking their places in Kansas, Siberia, Saskatchewan, and Argentina. In similar manner, lovely fabric of blues, greens, and silvers flecked with white became each ocean and sea, complete with whitecaps and bordering surf. A variety of blue-greens, all of crystal clarity, was transformed into inviting lakes, mysterious ocean depths, and entrancing underwater caverns.

My consciousness cleared, and I turned to look at Dr. Davidson. "What time is it?"

He raised his arm, glancing at his wrist watch. "It's 3:35."

We were silent a few moments. Then he asked, "Would you like some coffee?"

"No. No, thank you." At that moment coffee seemed far too mundane to be of the slightest interest. Besides I was sick that the day was passing so rapidly, thinking that time seems literally not to exist when under the drug.

Soon, as if I had willed it so, I was back in the world of beauty, confronted with the problem of producing rainbows. Weaving the silk for them seemed comparatively easy; only a few hundred were needed each day. There swung out across the sky striped luminous fabric like the finest veiling, akin to mist, at once both pastel and intense. With my fingertips I picked up bits of this lovely silk, pulling it out like chewing gum and making long, narrow rainbows which arched the whole of the heavens; shorter ones which I tucked neatly behind deep blue, gray, and purple storm clouds; and unusually wide ones, each drop sparkling like a gem, which I slipped under great, billowy clouds at one end; the other I buried in a glistening rain-soaked earth. The beauty was so intense that I sobbed as I smoothed each rainbow lovingly into place, thinking serenity must have been the warp and tranquillity the woof.

Making the flowers was a joyous and delightful experience. The first cocoon bolt to unroll was such a brilliant blue that I felt it was gaiety woven into fabric. Midway before my eyes it broke into tiny petals and, as if drawn by magnets, sped to waiting stems and formed a great field of dancing cornflowers. A bolt of red satin became a blanket of poppies scattered among the rows of white crosses over the graves in the fields of Flanders. They nodded happily as if to compensate for the tragedy buried there. Lovely striped material of every color changed into wild flowers along babbling streams, rocky nooks, and woods in bud, each scene so alluring that I wanted to become a part of it. Brilliantly plaid taffeta gave its riot of colors to quaint English gardens, to parks in every land, and to tropical jungles. Nor were snowflowers forgotten, or crimson hibiscus, dainty blue columbine, or azaleas.

A charming interlude came at this point. I felt I was a dandelion heralding spring, sunshine greeting sunshine. With brothers and sisters I lived on one attractive lawn after another, feeling both tremendously gay and fiercely hated. I wept brokenheartedly as boys cut me with lawn mowers and men sprayed me with weed killer. Children picked me and played, "He loves me, he loves me not," but their joy made my pain bearable. Other children blew my fragile seeds into the air, a wish for all seeds gone at once. Then I grew between two bricks near a basement window in a tenement district, and a crippled Italian woman discovered me, loved me, and did not hurt me, but her love became my pain. Next there appeared before me, so magnified as to cover the entire field of vision, a fourth of a gone-to-seed dandelion, translucent, bejeweled, and exquisitely lovely in design. Although I felt love for and oneness with every variety of flower, in spite of all the beauty I had seen, I loved the dandelions most tenderly.

As my mind started to clear, it seemed to me that Christ must have referred to the dandelions as well as to the insects by His phrase, "Unto one of the least of these." More than any other of the thousands of visions I had seen, the dandelions seemed to drive home the fact that beauty which was God was under our very noses at all times; yet we were mere humans who, having eyes, saw not.

CHAPTER 7

Among the Blest

I SAT UP, removed the sleep shade, and looked around the room, realizing regretfully that my third experience was probably half over. Then the sculptured head on the bookshelves smiled pleasantly, an act I interpreted to be a good omen.

"Are you ready for coffee now?" Dr. Davidson's question startled me. I had been so far behind the curtain I had forgotten he sat beside me.

"The coffee's cold," I replied. "I'd prefer bouillon."

"I'll see that it's hot, but I'll bring both."

The shaded electric light hurt my eyes; yet through the open door I could see much brighter sunshine which seemed soothing and inviting. Dr. Davidson brought two steaming cups, placed them on the low table at my side, and took his chair behind me.

The coffee was indeed hot, but the bouillon tasted much the better. As I drank it, I described visions I had seen, although my constantly chattering teeth made both drinking and talking difficult. When Dr. Davidson picked up the cups, I asked to be left alone again.

I had scarcely adjusted the sleep shade and pulled the

blanket over me when a gigantic plaid ribbon was undulating before me. It broke up and fluttered downward, looking like a sky full of autumn leaves; then the leaves became graceful swans, flamingos of lovely pink, and tropical birds of every hue. As each color changed to a bird or fowl, a vast montage of forests, lakes, and jungles passed slowly from left to right. Fish were formed of similar fabric but somewhat brighter in color and more luminous. All were exquisite in shape, delicacy of fin, and grace of movement. They swam above colorful coral beds and in and out of gardens of bright seaweed through light-saturated water sparkling with blue, green, and yellow phosphorescence.

Next I, as the sum total of all silkworms, felt impelled to beautify the highways of America. While I worked frantically to produce, spin, and weave the required silks, visions appeared of meetings being held in villages, towns, and cities, then of people planting flowering trees along every street, road, and highway. Mottled silk of merging colors billowed into view, broke into petals, and fell like gentle snow on magically matured trees: locust, cherry, almond, apple, flowering peach, jacaranda, catalpa, flaming eucalyptus, and many others. Every road sign, every dump heap was hidden. Then I passed down one road after another arched with endless and overwhelming beauty, and was welcomed by the fragrance of spring and soothed by a symphony of bees.

The silkworms received requests for so many fabrics that hundreds of back orders were always waiting to be filled. I could see them stacked on a desk, as if in a modern office. Awareness of these orders and the numerous difficulties in filling all of them seemed to come at once, making me feel as if an atomic bomb were about to explode inside my head. I had never expected to envy the slow-witted, but now with genuine sincerity I did.

I decided that the most urgent order was for silks to be used in producing blood for every living thing. There must be bright reds for arterial blood and purplish-red for venous blood; pale reds for the anemic, ill, and dying; and a brilliant crimson for newborn infants, the unusually vigorous, and persons who live at high altitudes. As the flawless silks swung out from the cocoon bolts, I felt that blood, as a symbol of all life, was infinitely precious. Beneath an ever-moving wealth of reds, there appeared a seemingly endless montage showing insects, fish, birds, animals, and peoples of all ages and races. As they passed slowly from left to right, there fell from the sky tiny bright threads which were replaced by increasingly larger ones until each living thing had received his quota of life-giving red.

Next I became part of the bloodstream of a wide variety of people and beasts. I could feel myself moving rapidly in darkness and pushed forward with each heartbeat. Successively I was aware of passing through a network of capillaries in the shoulder of a graceful gazelle as she loped across an African veld. For a second I explored the brain of Einstein, then the fin of a minnow. During a privileged moment I raced through the heart of Lincoln, feeling a reverence as if I were near God. Then I was in a wing of a tiny insect, the trigger finger of a murderer, and the leg of a fleet-footed fox.

During both my first and second LSD experiences, a feeling of oneness with all life had pervaded every cell of my body. This same feeling was now magnified a thousandfold and drove itself into my soul with such force that I expect to carry it to my grave. At that moment all life seemed so infinitely precious that I cried aloud. As I sobbed, I thought again, as I had many times before, that the visions of an LSD experience are relatively unimportant and merely serve as hooks upon which can be hung soul-shaking emotions.

The next order to be filled was for tears. The problems in design and the variety of silks required were so numerous it seemed this time that my head would surely burst. I ate mulberry leaves at fantastic speed and increased my body movements to convulsive proportions as I spun cocoons and enacted all parts of the silkworm cycle. Opalescent tears for light cheeks must be produced, topaz tears for yellow skin, smoky topaz for Negroes, and a different shading for every race and variation of complexion. There must be tears that dropped, tears that flowed, tears that remained swimming in eyes, and scarcely born tears that must be wiped away with dainty lace-bordered handkerchiefs. I must make far more of the fabric for tears that fall at night than for daylight tears. Moonlit tears for the white cheek must glisten with diamonds; for the yellow and brown cheeks, with gold. Textures too had to be considered: special tears to flow down wrinkled cheeks or into unshaved stubble or curly beards.

As magnificent silks meeting these qualifications filled the sky, sad faces of thousands of persons of every age and race appeared before me. I loved each so much I wanted to put comforting arms around every person, but I knew they needed solitude. Invisible to all, I put each tear in place with caressing tenderness. I gave transparent, pearl-shaped tears to a fat brown baby who lay watching a phosphorescent chameleon scurry among the fronds of a dried-palm thatch. After I had dropped them into his eyes, he stopped crying, and a smile covered his face. I knew that if more tears could fall, more smiles could follow; and I was saddened that the beauty of tears was so rarely appreciated. To me every tear showed the warmth, the humanness, and the alikeness of us all.

The wave passed, returning me to a world of dreary deadness. Immediately I longed to be back where I felt enveloped in beauty and rich colors, considering every minute away a wasted one. I stood unsteadily to stretch and quickly lay down again. After taking a fresh stick of gum to replace that which had served as mulberry leaves for the past two hours, I was soon lost in thought. Where did such amazing ideas come from? If I took LSD a hundred times or more, it would seem forever incredulous that so much beauty could be inside any person. The materials used for making tears still left me breathless: the sky full of near-transparent yet sparkling veiling, soft grays and beiges studded with diamonds and gold dust. Again arose the unshakable conviction that whatever beauty was inside me was likewise inside every human being. How could it be reached without the aid of a drug? Certainly I did not know the answer.

Such thoughts were interrupted by my being carried away from our world of familiar things. Three separate projects awaited me, and like all others, they were responsibilities which had to be executed immediately. I had to weave fabrics for the eyes, cheeks, and hair of all the peoples of the earth. Such omnipotence would be unforgivably conceited were it not for the fact that I, as a person, no longer existed and that I, as humanity at large or as silkworms, was aware of being wholly and completely an instrument of God.

After seemingly a thousand problems in design and shading had been considered, almost an endless variety of exciting colors and textures swept one after another across the sky. Too numerous for counting were the persons with kindly and interesting faces who came to receive their allotments. The silkworms made deprived persons particularly beautiful in compensation for their hurts. A Moslem street urchin in Casablanca was given rich red-tan cheeks, dark chocolate-brown eyes, and wavy black hair in which high lights glistened as in pools of water. A Finnish orphan girl received apple-red cheeks, eyes of the most intense sky blue, and hair of spun gold. A motherless Chinese baby was allotted jewel-bright black eyes and blue-black hair which shone like polished metal; and his yellow-pink cheeks were as soft as the silk from which they were made. These children seemed the embodiment of all children, and their charm and appeal revealed their inner beauty and drew me like a magnet. I felt that the brittle beauty of human beings which is appreciated lacked depth and meaning, whereas the true beauty inside every person—the beauty of the soul—usually went unnoticed.

Most of the remaining orders were for emotions or abstract concepts such as jealousy, envy, and hatred, each of which seemed impossible for anyone to design. "How can a cloth symbolize jealousy?" I asked intolerantly, angry to be given such a ridiculous task, yet thinking of an ugly yellow.

The queen of the silkworms answered vehemently, "No! No! An ugly cloth will never come from my looms." After a moment's silence, she spoke with great tenderness. "No one wants to be jealous. It is only when one's need for love is not fulfilled that jealousy occurs. Into this cloth must be woven much gold of love, some white silk of understanding, and brave red threads of courage for trying to obtain one's birthright."

There floated across the entire sky a vast expanse of soft orange-yellow veiling, inconceivably thin. Each dainty thread seemed to be lit from within by a light of extreme delicacy, giving it a luminosity which changed constantly as it waved and fell in graceful folds. As I watched in rapture, thinking there had never been such beauty, I admired the queen's tolerance and understanding, wondering how something which now seemed so clear could have been so vague a moment earlier.

There was too much work to be done for contemplation now. "Envy," I remarked, turning to another seemingly impossible task. "Surely you can't make something beautiful out of envy."

"Only the deprived are envious," the queen answered softly. "Fill their deprivations, and they are envious no more."

Again I functioned frantically for all silkworms until great swirls of new-growth green, like clouds of rapidly moving mist, filled the sky. In its phosphorescence were reflected exquisite lights and equally lovely shadows. Below these delicate clouds appeared a series of scenes. I saw women in bright evening gowns and men in formal attire dancing in an ornate ballroom, their faces covered with masks of veneer. There quickly followed a vision of Negroes sitting in front of a half-fallen-down shanty, playing battered homemade instruments and singing joyously into the night.

Next appeared a palatial home in Mexico City where richly dressed people sat around a banquet table with bored expressions on their faces. Then I watched a ragged peon carry wood across a dry, cactus-filled yard to his wife who tenderly suckled an infant as she stooped over a tiny fire; they exchanged smiles which made their love visible.

With sadness I observed a cocktail party at an exclusive country club where attractively clothed, jaded people were drinking more than they cared to. Last came a vision of a home on the wrong side of the tracks but where peace and serenity dwelt. Scarfs of new-growth green broke away from the clouds, floated gracefully to the sophisticated, the bored, and the jaded, and settled gently around the shoulders of these persons who are usually envied but are not the enviable.

Dr. Davidson came in. "It's five o'clock, and I have to see a patient. Could I do anything for you?"

"No, thank you."

"Would you like a sleeping tablet for tonight?"

A part of me realized that his question was prompted by kindness, and I managed another "No, thank you." Yet I felt furious and wanted to reply, "If you were watching colors more exquisite than anything you'd ever seen, would you take a sleeping tablet?" I felt that he was trying to deprive me of this beauty, hated him for it, and was glad when he closed the door.

Immediately I tried to plan a cloth symbolic of hatred and was thinking a shoddy black. Quickly the queen spoke again. "Hatred too is beautiful. No one ever hates unless he also loves. The two are one, inseparable."

Before me unfurled a great expanse of striking silk which contained much black but glittered with specks of the brightest gold. Then our earth, like a tremendous globe, revolved slowly before me while pieces of this material wafted downward and covered every continent with love and hate. An unseen hand turned over a large portion of each piece of silk, revealing gold fabric specked with black and indicating that the amount of love in the world was equal to or greater than the quantity of hate.

The queen's voice was soft and seemed filled with tolerance and wisdom. "The work of the world is done on hate," she explained. "All work done well is well done only when persons hate work done shoddily. Justice can exist only when injustice is hated, laws only when lawlessness is hated, and education only when ignorance is hated. Every improvement this world has ever known was brought about because someone hated intolerable conditions."

I remembered how Florence Nightingale hated the filth of

the Crimean War and had thus started the nursing profession; and how Clara Barton's hatred of the suffering during our Civil War had led to the founding of the American Red Cross. With tremendous clarity I could now see there was indeed beauty in hatred, and once more I sobbed for beauty which went unseen.

In this manner were filled many orders for fabrics symbolic of negative emotions. The two sides of the silks were invariably different but equally beautiful and showed the oneness of opposites. Cruelty and kindness were woven together, intolerance and tolerance, terror and security, brutality and compassion, and many other qualities and their opposites. The fabric of compassion contained many silver threads and was ablaze with jewels; and the compassion which filled me as I watched it was so great that it became pain, and my body shook with sobs.

Soon I lay trying to imagine how one could weave a silk showing criticism, feeling that the task was too big for me. Before me appeared a tremendous Paul Bunyan figure, seemingly made of putty, around which flew two dozen or more huge vultures. Each vulture dived, bit a piece of "flesh," and flew away with it, pulling it after him like a great strand of chewing gum. Then he let it go, and the rubbery putty sprang back into place. In this manner the vultures were continuously circling, diving, biting, pulling, and circling again. An unexplainable knowing told me that the scene symbolized each of us as our own severest critics. We viewed ourselves as ugly Paul Bunyans of faults, picking at ourselves like vultures, a striking contrast indeed to the intrinsic beauty I now saw in every human being. It seemed to me that to debase ourselves was no less than attempting to deprecate God Who made us.

Next there appeared many persons often the butt of jokes

or criticism: drunks, morons, spinsters, and others. As I watched, the queen spoke again, a touching tolerance evident in her voice: "One makes fun of others only when he sees in them qualities which he dislikes in himself. An already low opinion of self cannot stand the bruises of further blows. It is for this reason he must criticize others, although unknowingly he criticizes only himself. If people could only see their inner beauty, they'd have no need to criticize anyone."

Again I wept that still another form of beauty went unseen.

The next order was for silk which symbolized the soul. This time the fabric seemed to be woven of rainbows, sunrises, and sunsets. As I watched the radiant sky-wide magnificence, I cried aloud with agony almost beyond bearing, thinking that God had indeed made no mistakes in the people He had created.

The door opened, and Frank tiptoed in, almost as silent as a shadow. Another hour had passed, and it was time to go home. With difficulty I tried to stand, but to walk seemed impossible. The parking lot behind the building seemed miles away. "I can't make it. I can't!" I declared emphatically, regretting for the thousandth time that I had taken the 50 additional micrograms of the drug.

"Try," Frank encouraged, supporting my back with one arm and my elbow with the other.

With his help I managed a few faltering steps. As we reached the hall, Eve came out of the office. "Would you like some sleeping tablets?"

This time I was unable to suppress my anger. "Of course not! Why would any idiot want sleeping tablets?"

My attack startled her. "You might rest better tonight."

"No, but thank you anyway," I said weakly and without conviction. Months later I read that a psychiatrist, doing research on LSD, gave his patients sedation after a six-hour experience and for the two following days. Even then I was furious with such a destroyer of loveliness.

Walking was easier when we reached the open air, but I remained in a daze and, during the entire trip home, longed to be in bed. Since the thought of food brought immediate nausea, it was impossible to eat dinner. Although I was unable to stop my lip and jaw movements which indicated the eating of mulberry leaves, no visions appeared at this time. The moment I was in bed, shortly after 7 P.M., I became a silkworm larva nestled in the bliss of an infinitely soft cocoon. A feeling of unusual well-being and alertness continued for the next six hours, during which time visions appeared rapidly and almost continuously. Repeatedly I saw the modern office with its piles of orders still to be filled.

With renewed vigor, I resumed laying eggs, hatching, spinning cocoons, and doing all the work necessary to produce a silk symbolic of fault and blame. During the entire evening, as before, my whole body was constantly in rapid motion. Never once could I foresee what the silks would be like until they actually unfurled to fill the sky. This time sheer, near-transparent silk of inconceivable delicacy floated out like thistledown, broke into clouds of glistening mists, and quickly disappeared.

"There is no such thing as blame and fault," the queen explained quietly. "They are meaningless words. Every person does his best, and none does less than his best."

As silkworms collectively, I then had to design a fabric symbolizing death. Quickly I rejected the usual colors of mourning: the black of our culture and the white of the Orient. I felt that such material must contain colors symbolic of joy for release of pain, reward of work well done, eagerness for new experience, and gold for the nearness of God. There unfolded before me silk of such intense loveliness as to be indescribable; happiness must surely have been its loom, and bird song and lapping waters had been somehow woven into the fabric.

In similar manner the silkworms produced fabrics symbolic of war, illness, the downtrodden, and many, many other subjects. By their magic, they made each silk exquisite and each concept clear and understandable as it had never been before. While I was designing cloth representing downtrodden peoples, there appeared tragic Jewish pogroms: terrified persons fleeing from small villages as they were being pelted with stones, clods, and bricks; men with long beards and small black caps, utter helplessness written on their faces; sobbing women with great bundles on their backs, running, stumbling, and falling; innocent children crying, "Why? What have we done?" As I cried aloud, overcome with compassion, I felt I would see these scenes to my dying day.

While visions thus passed before me, claiming every instant of my attention, I was vaguely aware that Frank had lit the fire and put a bowl of fruit on a table by my bed. Now he learned over me, "Is there anything else I can do for you?"

I was out of "mulberry leaves" and at that moment felt willing to walk the two miles to the nearest store for more. "Yes," I answered. "Would you mind going to buy me more gum?"

With the strange intermingling of reality and fantasy, the chewing of gum seemed to me to be the actual eating of mulberry leaves. Not for a second is there make-believe in any LSD experience. About 1 per cent of my actual self seemed to observe while 99 per cent lived in the stark reality of the feelings attached to the visions. Now every task was of such seriousness that it weighed down my shoulders with responsibility.

As soon as Frank had gone, I lay considering a silk which

would show the quality of forgiveness. Then came a vision of Christ hanging on the cross, seemingly not four feet in front of me. Infinite sadness showed on His pain-racked face. Blue-black veins stood out on thin, deeply tanned arms and legs. His bony chest rose and fell in great rasping breaths. I saw the muscles in each arm and wrist contract as He attempted again and again to cup His bleeding hands into a plea for forgiveness, pulling at the nails which pierced the palms. I wondered what other similarly tortured men would do. Then on different crosses hung men of many nationalities, one after another, each screaming blasphemous oaths. I cringed before their agonized yells. When I looked up again, Christ was once more before me, still on the cross. Then came His voice, tender and pleading, "Father, forgive them; for they know not what they do."

Behind the cross, covering the whole of the heavens, unfurled silk of the purest white, the purity of forgiveness, and of the brightest gold, the gold of love. The constantly moving fabric fell into graceful folds, giving off sparkling rays like a setting sun.

As I sobbed uncontrollably, it occurred to me that His phrase, "they know not what they do," was as important as His plea for forgiveness. Since all of our actions are unconsciously motivated, this phrase seemed to apply daily to every one of us, making the need for forgiveness a constant need. Then I saw that the silkworms had made the pure white of forgiveness similar to the off-white of understanding because to understand is to forgive.

Frank brought the gum and, knowing I wished to be alone, left quickly, saying he would help our son with his homework.

Instantly I was deep under the drug again, hundreds of ideas still seeming to come at one time. My heart went out to persons mentally ill who are said to have lost their ability to filter thoughts singly through the conscious mind.

For what must have been hours, I, as the sum total of all silkworms, made materials representing each race and many individuals of each race. Again and again silks of overpowering beauty filled the heavens. All were variegated, all were different, and yet all were amazingly alike. The fabric symbolizing Abraham Lincoln contained more gold threads than most; Gandhi's cloth showed much silver of compassion; and Booker T. Washington's glowed like opals as the exquisite off-white threads of understanding made marked contrast to his dark skin.

It seemed strikingly clear that we were all God's children and, despite variations in talents and accomplishments, that no person was better than another. Every fabric, like every individual of every race, contained both strong threads and weak ones and all negative emotions and all positive ones. Each showed the gold of love and God. This time I wept not only because of an overwhelming feeling of oneness with all who live but a new soul-shaking appreciation of the inner beauty, either seen or potential, of all humanity.

Next my thoughts turned to the use of gold as a symbol of God. In succession, I saw the gold-leaf-covered domes of St. Peter's and St. Sophia's cathedrals; gold-decorated Moslem mosques and Shinto and Buddhist temples; gold statues of Christ and Buddha and gold crosses on churches; and the devout of many lands, fingering gold prayer beads.

The queen spoke again. "Everyone knows that gold symbolizes God. It makes no difference whether He is called Allah, Brahma, or any other name. He is still the same God."

Then appeared a series of puzzling scenes in which gold was not symbolic of God. I watched pirates steal gold from the early Incas and the churches in old Peru and load it on picturesque sailing ships. Next I saw pirate chests on sandy ocean floors spilling precious stones and gold coins into the water's luminous greens and yellows, almost as brilliant as the coins and jewels themselves. A prostitute at a bar in the tropics slipped stolen gold coins into a pocket under her black, lace-bordered garter. Midas appeared, counting tremendous piles of coins. Lastly an Alaskan miner, hugging a gold nugget in a gloved fist, trudged through deep snow against a cruel blizzard. Before my eyes he sank to the ground, died, and was quickly covered by snow. I lay frantically chewing mulberry leaves, trying to solve this inconsistency.

Then with her voice filled with sadness, the queen explained, "Even today people worship many gods. The beauty of the real God, like so much other beauty, is rarely seen."

On the top now were orders for silks symbolizing crime, delinquency, insanity, and murder. Before me passed a vast montage of every type of crime and hurt: holdups, gun firings, knifings, stabbings, stealings, and burglaries, children being cuffed, slapped, kicked, and beaten; rapings, incests, and houses of prostitution; young girls, in overcrowded slums and wealthy homes alike, attempting abortions; and babies being rejected, hated, and left tied alone in cribs.

On and on came these visions of people whose rejections, frustrations, and deprivations had led them to tragedy, causing me to sob heartbrokenly. It seemed to me that they were the truly hurt and that I had reached a new plateau of understanding them. Then I spun cocoons with frantic speed, swinging my hips in wide circles and enacting all stages of silk making seemingly at once. This time the silkworms wished to weave a special cocoon around each deprived person. These cocoons had to be particularly soft and lovely to compensate for sadness, harshness, and ugliness; only the threads of love, warmth, joy, and happiness could be used in making them. It was as if the queen wished to hold each of these persons in her womb until he could be reborn with the prerequisites to assure a fulfilling life.

Then I produced silk after silk symbolic of abstract ideas, the meanings of which I had often searched for blindly and falteringly. Suddenly, as if a veil were lifted, by the time such fabrics were woven, meaning after meaning became strikingly clear.

My next problem was to weave materials symbolic of femininity and masculinity. In rapid sequence there appeared an appealing baby boy in diapers, a runabout in starched rompers, a ready-for-Sunday-School child in Lord Fauntleroy suit, a Huck Finn in ragged denims, an adolescent in acolyte robe, a teenager in shorts, and on through the flannels, tweeds, and wools of manhood to old age. Then appeared a rerun, but this time by the side of each was woman: the loving mothers of infant and runabout; a proud woman in Easter hat watching from church pew her acolyte son; and on through woman's lifespan to a gentle, white-haired grandmother sitting beside her aging mate.

Before me I saw a great pendulum, seemingly attached to the very dome of the sky, its arc reaching from horizon to horizon. As it moved slowly from left to right, thirty or more visions were superimposed upon it: women with no rights, downtrodden in every land; Susan B. Anthony leading a parade of shouting rebels carrying banners; Carrie Chapman Catt preaching on street corners, demanding women's rights from all who passed; and Emmeline Pankhurst being thrown in jail. Then came liberation: veils dropped from the lovely faces of Moslem women; American women competed with men in factories and offices and for executive positions; and some women wore trousers and had their hair cut like men.

The queen spoke again: "What woman has gained in freedom, she has more than lost in femininity."

Then across my vast field of vision there appeared, side by side, two great quantities of cloth. One was of heavy texture and rich dark colors. Although it was made entirely of silk, it seemed to contain wools, denims, and much tweed, and it gave the feeling of power, strength, and dignity. Beside it was a gauzy veiling of changeable silk showing many pastel colors which varied constantly, as if they were dancing; sunshine yellows symbolic of joy and soft pinks representing warmth predominated and blended together as in a Peace rose. The total display was fascinating to me; yet the most striking note was the completeness with which the two materials complemented each other.

The wave passed, and for a time I watched the reflections from the flames in the fireplace play upon the ceiling. As I lay thinking of the theme of this experience, I knew that it was the beauty of God Who is in all things, even those as tiny as an insect's wing or as common as a dandelion; that intrinsic beauty, which had been hidden deep within myself and was now so gloriously revealed to me, is a portion of God; and that this God-given inner beauty is in every human being. We need only to look about us and within ourselves to see Him.

I could see now that it was not a lack of appreciation of beauty itself which had made me so sad during the first part of the experience. Beauty had been merely a symbol for God, and it was my failure to recognize Him which had caused the sadness. Furthermore, I was convinced that man alone, turning away from God, had created the ugliness in himself and in the world. The awareness which had come at the end of the second experience, that God was in every nook and cranny of the universe, was now so tremendously increased and so richly fulfilling that a great reverence enfolded me, as if faith held me in her arms.

After a time, my entire body began to shake convulsively, every muscle struggling as if it were bound with heavy ropes. The intense struggle, which must have lasted ten minutes or longer, seemed to symbolize a particularly difficult emergence from a cocoon and to signify a rebirth into greater understanding and a greater appreciation of God.

Finally there remained only one order, a fabric which symbolized love. As I produced threads of dazzling gold, Christ's demand, "Love thy neighbour as thyself," seemed far too modest. At that moment there surged within me a tremendous feeling of love for all humanity. Next the words of a song flashed through my mind: "The love in your heart was not put there to stay. Love is not love till you give it away." I thought of the millions of years love had been evolving, and wondered how many more millenniums would have to pass before love totally without selfishness could be achieved by most of us.

Then the queen spoke for the last time: "Only love can fill the vacuum in every heart. Love is God; the two are one; and love which is God is beauty in itself, a beauty which is also God. When you think you are hungry for love, it is, in reality, God you are longing for."

Her words caused me to feel again a wonderful oneness with all humanity, for in the universal struggle for love, we are alike. It seemed to me that when a person once accepts love, not only his family and friends feel it but everyone who is near him; like a noonday sun, he gives off rays and warmth to all alike; and that our recognition of this radiance of love was shown by the tired cliché, "All the world loves a lover."

At last the work was finished. The wonderful warmth of love still pervaded every cell of my body, and around me I could feel the soft silkiness of a cocoon. Then sweeping across the heavens came the gold of love and God, rich beyond imagining. As it moved from left to right with unbelievable magnificence, it revealed one golden landscape after another, each vibrant with splendor. Across skies of the most delicate white gold there seemed to float clouds of golden mist. Great gold mountains reached their arms to heaven, their peaks glittering in golden sunlight. Burnished gold nestled in the shadows, and the softest of golden vapors caressed the slopes. Rivers of spun gold appeared to flow tranquilly past golden grainfields awaiting harvest, while golden trees swayed and bowed their heads in reverence. God, here symbolized by gold, was again shown to pervade all things. So overcome was I by the loveliness before me and the feelings which swept over me that I wept without restraint, knowing that, within my heart, love and beauty and God had become one.

The silkworms had woven their masterpiece. Now it was their turn to nestle into the softness of their cocoons, while I, like the queen herself, knew I was among the blest. She had opened my eyes both to beauty such as this world has never seen and to God.

CHAPTER 8

The Same God

Terror, which had curdled my blood at the onset of the first LSD session, which had caused me to feel frozen at the beginning of the second, and which had delayed the third for one and a half hours, dominated the entire fourth experience.

Dr. Henry Hill, who had been my monitor during Pegasus' flight among the planets, was interested in knowing whether an LSD experience would be influenced when it followed an hour of psychotherapy. Just as the objective of college is intellectual development, the purpose of psychotherapy is emotional development with selfless love as its goal. Yet to be capable of such love, one must become truly selfless. To let go so completely causes such feelings of helplessness and vulnerability to emotional hurts that it is a terrifying thing, even though much of it remains unconscious. For example, it is this same fear of letting go which makes it impossible for many persons to be hypnotized or to have rich drug experiences.

When, immediately after an hour's psychotherapy, on February 8, 1960, I went to Dr. Janiger's office, fear had already been intensified by the therapy and was increased to terror by the knowledge that LSD would literally force me to let go. This terror, remaining partly unconscious, first showed itself by the visions instead of by my feelings. Nevertheless, at noon when Dr. Janiger gave me 150 micrograms of the drug, I felt weak, shaky, and anxious.

One of the ways we unknowingly defend ourselves against devastating emotions can be summarized by the statement: "If I don't let myself feel anything, I can't feel something unpleasant." I unconsciously used this defense throughout the first half of the fourth experience. When we keep our emotions on the surface, however, we are like floating bubbles which never see the beauty of the depths. Even in the absence of deep feelings, my mind took off on a tangent over which I had not the slightest control and thousands of visions appeared, their content invariably light.

Soon after I took the drug, Dr. Davidson made me comfortable in his office, placed a sleep shade over my eyes, and started the music. I was still consumed with anxiety, and the melody seemed so full of unpleasant yearnings that I immediately asked him to turn it off. I definitely wanted to be alone and told him so. Although I was far from being aware of it at the time, it was later obvious to both of us I had feared that either the music or something Dr. Davidson might say would plunge me into deeper feelings than I was willing to cope with. The doctor told me he would work in the adjoining room where I might call him if I wished.

He had scarcely closed the door when I drew my lower lip into my mouth as far as I could. Simultaneously the upper part of my body started to sway, a movement which continued throughout much of the experience. I seemed to have bright, beady eyes with a cap pulled down over them. With quick movements, I turned my head from side to side as if wanting nothing to escape my glance. Then clarity came, and

I saw I was a hooded cobra about ten feet long. So impressive were the flowing grace and striking beauty of my body that it did not occur to me I was deadly poisonous. Furthermore I now felt happy-go-lucky, marvelously secure, and as if the world were mine. Although I was definitely feminine, I seemed to be somewhat of a playboy variety of cobra.

I spent considerable time admiring my luminous skin which had markings of pale green, soft brown, and lemon yellow, the whole shining like sequins lit from within. The lower part of my body was coiled. My head and some four feet of length were held upright and swayed to the rhythm of drums beaten by nude, Polynesian men. I was watching a group of Balinese women wearing only short brilliantly flowered skirts and dancing with jerky, angular movements. We were in a grove of coconut palms bordering a sleepy lagoon. Soon I slithered on past grass huts around which swarms of children were playing. Although the year was about 600 B.C., the island seemed badly overcrowded, and I kept repeating in Balinese to every adult I met, "If you people don't stop having so many children, you'll have a problem of overpopulation here some day."

For a time I lay on a beach watching men pack outrigger canoes for voyages into the unknown. I worried because the tapa cloth they carried to catch drinking water would be useless in areas without rain and their spears would be valueless when no fish could be found. Many such adventures, I realized, would be unsuccessful, but visions showed parties arriving at Samoa, Tahiti, the Philippines, and numerous other islands.

My home, I knew, was in India, where I had lived for hundreds of years. I waited impatiently for the monsoons to blow northwest, saying intolerantly, "One is forced to plan travel far in advance." Eventually I boarded a large log and slept out the journey to my native land. Again in a game of prostrate charades, I acted out the movements of swimming to and climbing onto the log, sleeping during the trip, and all later activities of the cobra's adventures as they occurred. Before the day was over, I had so frequently rotated my hips in the snake-like fashion of coiling, lurched the upper part of my body into the "air," moved my head about with rapid jerks, and glided so rhythmically with my entire body swaying from side to side that I felt I had become quite adept at snake life.

Soon I found myself in a jungle. I slid along leisurely for several yards; then to get my bearings I coiled and quickly lifted my body to different heights through layers of luxuriant green, frequently repeating the procedure. Each time I looked down on verdant masses of beautiful foliage sparkling with freshness, raindrops still clinging to the leaves.

Once I came face to face with a lion which had briers in his mane. As he turned and ran, I scoffed contemptuously, still with a feeling of utter security, "King of the jungle. Ha!" A moment later I discovered his mate nursing her cubs and quickly decided not to mix with her. "An irritable lot, those mother lions," I remarked with disgust. After passing several leopards, a tiger, and many deer, I rested beside a river and watched rhinoceroses, hippopotamuses, and water buffalos standing shoulder deep in the current. As the buffalos swished flies from their backs, their wet tails threw sprays of water into the air. A dozen or more crocodiles sunned on the bank, and occasionally a few crawled slowly in or out of the river. "A lazy bunch of good-for-nothings," I said, shrugging as I turned back to the jungle. Next I stood on my tail toe-dancer fashion and watched chattering monkeys and brilliantly colored birds hopping among the high branches of a massive banyan tree.

As I moved on, an elephant almost stepped on me. Instantly I coiled and sprang angrily to face her. "Watch where you're going, you lumbering beast," I hissed. Then I noticed a white baby elephant behind her. "Keep him hidden," I warned her quickly. "People around here think white elephants are sacred. They'll make his life miserable."

I noticed giant dragonflies flitting about and decided that they would make an appetizing breakfast. Their slender, metallic-appearing bodies showed a mottling of aqua-blue, foliage-green, and chocolate-brown colors. Their graceful wings, which were limpid and gauzy thin, sparkled as if their surface were set with tiny jewels. After I had sprung lightly from one tasty dragonfly to another, I decided that fish would make an appropriate second course. Miraculously I found myself in an aqueous paradise of ever-changing sunlit blues, yellows, and pale greens. Around me were swimming dozens of small fish of graceful shapes and luminous colors. For several moments I watched a tiny cornflower-blue fish which had huge, almost transparent blue-bordered fins. The infinite delicacy with which he moved his fins fascinated me. Suddenly he saw me and jerked to instant immobility, his black eyes becoming magnified into large marbles of terror. "You poor little thing!" I exclaimed. "I wouldn't put that much fear in my stomach." Slowly I swam toward a meal of phosphorescent green plankton which drifted gracefully on the surface of the sea, rays of bright sunlight filtering through it.

After the wave passed, I felt so much my normal self that the LSD seemed as innocent as a slice of toast. Without difficulty I walked to the adjoining room and watched a young woman splash great blobs of color across a canvas as she glanced frequently at the kachina doll. Soon I returned and asked Dr. Davidson if I might have a cup of coffee.

"Unless you want it very much, it probably wouldn't be

wise," he answered, looking somewhat concerned. "There's too much danger of vomiting."

Later I suspected, as Dr. Davidson did at the time, that I was unconsciously attempting to use this means of getting rid of the drug. I felt no disappointment, however, but lay down, pulled the blanket around me, and put the sleep shade back over my eyes.

Soon I was a cobra again, this time on land. I explored village after village only a few miles apart, consisting of mud huts thatched with long, dried grasses. Hordes of children played near the huts while women clad in white saris gathered around wells and men worked the small outlying fields. In each village I said repeatedly to men and women alike, "If you don't stop having so many children, you're going to have a problem with overpopulation some day." I felt proud of being able to use the various native dialects.

At times I made my way through dust three inches deep, and at other times I wallowed through oozy mud or swam puddles, thinking that 400 inches of rainfall a year was entirely too much. Beside a winding stream which ran through a clearing, I found women washing clothes by pounding them against rocks. "You should buy a combination electric washer and drier," I told them, disgusted with their primitive methods.

Before I could reach the next village, I already knew what had happened by the droves of vultures swarming overhead. I looked into one hut after another and saw several corpses in each. "Everyone dead of starvation and no one left to burn the bodies," I remarked sadly. "The crops are so heavy everyone's getting fat in that village four miles south of here. What a pity the people haven't built roads." I glided on, shaking my head and talking to myself. "Every time the Americans ship them wheat, they multiply until the next famine. Then a thousand die instead of the hundred who would have died if wheat hadn't been sent them. What cruelty is done in the name of kindness!"

Death was all too familiar to me; I had lived in India since the Aryans streamed through the Khyber Pass. Then visions of the Aryan migrations appeared. Fair-skinned women wearing skirts of fur and bearded men with fur around their loins galloped down from the foothills, their long matted hair streaming behind them and the snow-capped mountains towering in the distance. Next I watched them conquering mud villages of helpless dark-skinned shepherds, stealing women and sheep alike. Later I saw them gather around campfires at night and listen to their priests tell stories from the Vedas. I wondered how they kept all their gods apart: the fire-gods, the sun-gods, and the gods of the seasons, rivers, mountains, and forests.

With good reason, I felt proud of the people of India. I was well aware they had been weaving beautiful cloth, making public parks, conducting state governments, and writing the Vedas in Sanskrit when the peoples of Europe still lived in caves. Many visions passed before me: the weavers, park builders, officials conducting meetings under large trees, and white-clad persons writing on bark with plant juices.

Realism took over, and I lay disgusted with myself, thinking the experience was nothing more than an insipid travelogue. I recalled a psychiatrist friend telling us of a colleague who had given the usual dose of LSD to a somewhat stiff, cold, and self-possessed man. Since there had been no reaction, he had kept giving more of the drug until the total dose reached 500 micrograms.

"Then what happened?" our friend had asked his colleague.

"Nothing. That doughhead just sat there."

The story had seemed humorous at the time, but now that I was the doughhead, it was not funny. Yet there seemed no possible way to change the course of the experience.

Soon I was back in India, this time in a garden surrounding a white palace, a place I realized was my favorite haunt. Before me was an ornate palace with its garden of playing fountains, tiers of blooming flowers, and, at a distance, masses of huge trees. Brightly colored birds flew about among the blossoms of flowering shrubs.

Suddenly a group of servants trotted down a path toward heavy gates. I followed them through narrow streets and watched them drive away beggars, the poor, and the sick. Back in the courtyard, every servant came to attention, then bowed to the ground. Before me came the same little white elephant I had seen in the jungle. This time his back was covered with a bright, orange-red blanket bordered in gold. Upon him rode the little prince, Siddhartha, dressed in spotless white robes and turban.

"That poor little elephant," I exclaimed disapprovingly. "Shouldn't have his trunk off his mother's tail yet. Men in white jackets should come get old Prince Gautama. Little Siddhartha will never amount to a hill of beans, protected like that." I shook my head in disgust. "The problems of the children show the neuroses of the parents." With great emphasis, I added, "I raise my children the way they should be raised."

The scene shifted to a sandy, sun-drenched beach where I quickly dug a depression, laid soft-shelled eggs in it, and covered them with a few light swishes of my tail, my own body making egg-laying and tail-swishing motions. I stayed nearby and watched carefully until brilliantly colored little snakes wiggled from their shells and slipped into the water. With maternal pride I remarked, "They'll learn to fight their own battles and grow up to be nice, self-reliant snakes."

Soon I was back in Prince Gautama's garden, where day after day I watched as the streets were cleared and the little prince went for his ride. "That poor little kid'll never amount to a hill of beans," I kept repeating. With mounting disgust, I resumed traveling.

Immediately I was in China, watching scores of small children help men and women harvest grain. After I had warned the parents about the dangers of overpopulation, I went on to an ornate home of a Chinese overlord. Here women were binding a baby's feet. "I don't see how you can stand to hear her cry month after month," I declared vehemently. "Besides, beauty's in the heart, not in the feet." As an aside, I added, "That's a strange chastity belt. A woman can't walk well enough to get away from her husband."

Next I was in Siam observing small-boned girls with bright cloth wrapped around their hips stir beige material in huge vats of magnificently colored vegetable dyes. "In Europe they don't even know how to weave yet," I told them, again feeling a pride in ancient Oriental culture.

Dr. Davidson came quietly into the room. "Would you care to tell me what's happening?" After he had listened to a quick synopsis, he said, "Go deep inside yourself."

With instant anger I resented his remark. He had appeared to be a pleasant person when he had entered the room, but now before me stood a devil wearing tights made of bright, orange-red fish scales. He was increasing my rage by punching me with a black, short-pronged pitchfork. Fortunately he left without realizing that I, as a deadly cobra, was coiled ready to strike him.

Instead I sang out happily, "*Que será, será.* Whatever will be, will be. The future's not ours to see. *Que será, será.*" Then I added with cocky smugness, "Everyone has his own rate of growth."

Despite my violent reaction, I glided down, down, down into a deep cave. It was lit with ultraviolet light which showed a floor, walls, and ceiling formed of huge, jagged boulders. These massive rock formations glowed with rich phosphorescent greens, yellows, blues, and purples. Although the intensity of the colors was beautiful, the cave was so lonely that I experienced a few moments of extreme discomfort. Quickly I rationalized that the lack of activity made the place uninteresting and left as rapidly as I could.

I decided to go traveling again and soon found myself in Australia, face to face with a duck-billed platypus. "You're the funniest-looking beast I ever saw," I told her. "Fur like an animal, pouch like a kangaroo, feet and mouth like a duck. You can't decide what you want to be. 'The greatest sin of the spirit is indecision.' Besides, how can you kiss with a mouth like that?"

The platypus dived into the water, and I returned to India to see what had happened to Siddhartha.

Prince Gautama was still allowing his son, considerably larger now, to see nothing ugly. Arrangements had been made for the prince's marriage, and I wanted to talk to the child who was to be his bride. Before me appeared a beautiful girl, slight, with huge chocolate-brown eyes and hair so black that its gloss was almost navy blue. She wore a gold-bordered white scarf and sari of lovely sheer material.

"How can Siddhartha know what happiness is?" I asked her. "No one can experience happiness without knowing unhappiness first. Besides, he'll never amount to . . ."

With wisdom beyond her years, she turned aside, ignoring my remarks.

Visions then showed the prince after he was married and his son was born. On the day the servants forgot to clear the streets, I watched him closely as he discovered a beggar whose bones protruded through parchment-like skin. His next glance fell on a man covered with open sores where crawled thousands of maggots, and lastly on a corpse lying in a gully. That night, after his father had had the servants put to death, I watched Siddhartha alternately weeping and moaning as he paced back and forth in a richly decorated room lit by a single wick in a saucer of oil. A few days later I saw him talking to the holy men. With a heavy heart I watched him slip away into the night without kissing his wife or son good-by, remarking for the last time, "He'll never amount to a hill of beans." One final vision showed Siddhartha living with the holy men in a cave.

Then I seemed my normal self again. I got up and walked around the room, surprised that I felt the drug so little. I was still disgusted with the light tone the experience had taken and thought of it as a waste of time. The variety in which the visions were cast, however, fascinated me. Except for the breakfast episode and the lighted sequins of the cobra's skin and the devil's suit, which were as fanciful as my interplanetary travels, the remainder of the visions seemed unbelievably real. The jungle of wild animals, the poverty-stricken villages, the corpse-filled huts, and the thick mud still made me shudder.

I lay down and had scarcely pulled the blanket around me when I was again a hooded cobra. This time a dark Hindu carried me in a wicker basket, usually keeping my body covered with a filthy cloth. We visited bazaars in city after city. I would coil beside him, and soon my neck and head were moving to the rhythm of his small flute. Whenever he stopped playing, I looked around at the trays of carved ivory, perfumes, and ornate jewelry and admired the displays of wool, silks, beautiful rugs, and steel weapons.

Like a football spectator rooting for both teams, I particularly enjoyed listening to the traders from Egypt, Greece, Persia, Babylonia, and all parts of the then-known world as they haggled over prices. Next my attention turned to the veiled women and the servants of the wealthy who bought tropical fruits, strange-looking vegetables, sugar cane, flowers, curry, and dozens of varieties of grains and seeds. In this manner, scores of years passed.

Next there came before me caravans of camels heavily laden with huge bundles. Mustard-colored dust was so thick that it seemed to be matted into the camels' hair and quantities of it were in the corners of their eyes, making the poor beasts look miserable. Dust also covered the swarthy faces of the drivers and had sifted into their curly beards and uncombed black hair which hung to their shoulders. I could hear these drivers swearing at their tired camels so continuously that it appeared to be their favorite pastime. With the sun scorching my back, the hot sands burning my belly, and clouds of dust almost strangling me, I followed a caravan until its load was packed onto a small sailing vessel at a port on the Mediterranean.

Soon the city of Alexandria lay before me, its white buildings markedly contrasting with the blue waters of the Mediterranean. Then I noticed a huge, flat-roofed building surrounded by colonnades of pillars which I seemed to recognize as the ancient library of Alexandria. "All of Carnegie's libraries combined couldn't compare with this one," I remarked. "The knowledge of the entire world, including the secrets of Atlantis, is collected here." A flash of flames suddenly filled my field of vision as the library burned, and I knew the darkness of the Middle Ages was only a few centuries away. I commented sadly, "O'Leary's cow didn't do half that much harm."

After several more years of travel I eventually returned to

India to find that the Maurya emperors had come and gone. Asoka was in power. I learned he was a disciple of someone they called the Enlightened One, the Buddha. It seemed impossible to believe people were referring thus to Siddhartha Gautama. "Everyone makes mistakes," I declared, both philosophically and incredulously.

For a time I watched a great road Asoka had built. Before me were the wells he had had dug and the fruit trees he had had set out so that travelers could have water, shade, and food; the herb gardens to be used for medicines; and the great stone pillars inscribed with Buddhist teachings. The road, although wide, was constantly jammed with travelers on foot and on burros and with camel caravans, ox carts, and shepherds driving their flocks. Other men rode on horseback, in chariots, and on elephants with the bright curtains of their howdahs flapping in the breeze. Along the side of the road heavily veiled women, carrying large water jars and trays of fruit on their heads, glided like swift shadows through the dusty haze.

When clarity came, I kept wondering where the material for the visions could have possibly come from. I was sure that I knew almost nothing of the history of India, and certainly I had never been in the country. I could recall having read only two novels whose settings were there: *The Rains Came* by Louis Bromfield, and another whose title and author had completely escaped me. The experience was so convincing, however, that I felt I had actually lived in India and knew every part of the country well. Even weeks later when a guest told of her extensive travels throughout India, her words could not have seemed more familiar if she had been speaking of the small town where I grew up.

As a cobra, I resumed my travels and wandered on throughout the country until some three hundred years had passed. Then I wanted to see a king who, I had heard, had been born in Judea. Again I crossed southern Asia by caravan, this time hitch-hiking inside a camel's pack. In a small flat-roofed building made of stones and plaster, I found Him, a boy of perhaps ten, helping His father and brothers build a cart of rough boards. He was shaping holes into which wooden pegs were to be driven. From His slender shoulders hung a loose garment of coarsely woven wool. To me He seemed an ordinary child, although His face was more serious than most.

"At least they aren't spoiling Him as they did Siddhartha," I commented approvingly.

During the following years I watched Him with interest and felt that He was a gentle and kind man but not an extraordinary one. After He had revealed His wisdom by His teachings, I was as surprised as the people who asked, "Is He not the carpenter's son?"

Ancient city after ancient city next appeared before me. "The civilizations I have seen rise and fall," I said with a sigh. "I remember Nineveh as a small village, then as a glorious city. She disappeared so completely that for years archeologists thought she had never existed. So it is with China. I can't even remember all the dynasties any more."

Several hundred years were spent pleasantly in world traveling. While I was visiting Arabia, there appeared before me a dark-skinned boy with huge, serious eyes. He was herding sheep and camels in an inviting oasis. Date palms grew along a tiny stream which bubbled out of the sandy soil. Next I saw him at a fair in Mecca where tents of striped materials were pitched in a great square. Inside the square were herds of camels, sheep, and goats and booths in which were displayed the caravan-brought riches of East and West. Nearby there hung for sale fly-covered carcasses and thick-piled Persian rugs.

Again I listened while traders, seemingly of every nationality, haggled over prices. The milling crowd was predominantly Arabs who were clothed in white or striped materials with matching headdresses. Orators shouted to anyone whose attention they could claim. I watched the young Arabian as he listened intently to an orator telling of the life and teachings of Christ and to another exalting the God of the Jews. Somehow I knew he was Mohammed, but he seemed such an ordinary person I could never have guessed that he would be the founder of a new religion.

Zigzagging on through time, I again visited the Orient and the Middle East and went on to Turkey, Greece, and Italy, an almost endless number of visions passing before my eyes. This time, everywhere I went I found gold-adorned Buddhist temples, mosaic-trimmed Moslem mosques, massive-domed cathedrals, and hundreds of beautiful churches. Again and again the thought came to my mind: "Billions of people have lived and died; yet out of this tremendous mass of humanity, three seemingly ordinary men have changed the lives of all of the rest. Only three men, and billions of others."

Reality came, but the impact of the visions left me deep in thought. Although we in our culture accept the holiness of Christ as the only Son of God, perhaps an equal number of people believe Mohammed to be God's only prophet. I recalled that even Christians and Moslems combined still formed a small minority. Billions more people have lived and still live convinced that the Buddha, Siddhartha Gautama, was the most important representative of God ever to live on earth.

I knew that the teachings of these three great religious leaders were amazingly similar. Regardless of the small differences in the religions they founded, it seemed to me that each faith was essentially valid. The really important fact, I felt convinced, was one which should never be lost sight of: the three founders each embraced the same God, and every one of their billions of followers worshiped Him.

CHAPTER 9

Even unto the End

IT WAS already beginning to get dark, and the sands of my fourth experience had half run out. The marvelous security I had felt since the onset still held, a marked contrast to the fears which had gnawed me. Not until days later did it occur to me that, of all animals, a cobra is perhaps best equipped to cope with dangers, and I marveled that my brain had selected this characterization to still my fears. Fortunately for me, not a single mongoose had appeared. But now my thoughts were on the similarities of the world's religions, and even the cobra was temporarily forgotten.

Dr. Davidson came into the room, took the chair beside the davenport, and asked, "What's been going on?"

With his entrance, my mood had shifted to one bordering on gaiety. "I'm having a marvelous time!" I answered enthusiastically. "The best traveling I've ever done, and certainly the cheapest." Then I attempted to tell him everything I had seen, talking rapidly and not wanting to stop.

Dr. Davidson was well aware that I was unconsciously trying to hold the floor so that he would have no chance to say anything I did not want to hear.

"Don't waste LSD by talking," he interrupted. Then his voice became stern, and he added with commanding emphasis, "Get down into your feelings!"

Again I saw him as a devil. His glowing fish scales were a deep maroon this time, and a long forked tail of brilliant red swished behind him as he left the room. In a flash soul-shaking emotions took over, each seeming more intense than the previous one. I broke into loud, uncontrollable weeping. First I loathed Dr. Davidson. Then the projected feeling came home where all hatred belongs: in the heart of the hater. Although I was no longer the cobra, her venom filled me, and I loathed myself for not being able to feel during five hours or more of the experience. I knew that, as long as I was unwilling to feel the depths of terror, I would be unable to know the profundity of love; and that if even one negative emotion were held back, every positive emotion would likewise be kept prisoner.

My loud cries were suddenly frozen by terror. The cobra was hissing angrily not ten inches from my face. I was as terrified as if a cobra were actually attacking me; to me, she *was* a live cobra, and she *was* attacking me. Furthermore she continued to attack me during the two longest hours I have ever lived.

"You're afraid of your feelings, you coward," she hissed venomously. "You borrowed my skin, and you've been showing off how much you know, you despicable smart aleck. I'm a decent self-respecting snake, and I want nothing to do with you. Ssss! Sssss! Ssssss!"

Fear paralyzed me at the first sight of her. For what seemed an eternity, my body felt like stone at many degrees below freezing. Although the luminous reptile was brilliant before me, now all else was darkness.

The cobra had no intention of leaving me alone. Her

beady eyes gleamed with anger as she continued hissing at me, her head moving constantly, now even nearer my face. "What did you see when Dr. Davidson told you to look deep inside yourself? Nothing but cold stone! Even the light was phony. Turn off the light, and what's left? Cold unpierceable darkness! There's only one thing which can make a heart glow with warmth, and that's love."

My throat muscles were like steel bands, so constricted with fear that I could not answer.

A note of utter contempt surged into her hissing. "You couldn't stand to look at the cave long. You found it lonely inside yourself didn't you? What is it you're lonely for? Love, isn't it? There's only one source of love, and that's God."

The feelings of stoniness and coldness were already overpowering, and now was added a bottomless loneliness. Even these emotions could not crowd out the choking horror. My body was racked with sobs, and the nearness of the cobra's deadly poison made me writhe constantly in terrorized agony.

"Every time you've felt unloved, you've looked to other human beings, like a baby turning to its mother," she sneered disdainfully. "A mature adult looks to God for love, not to another person. God's love is everywhere. There's never been a deficiency of His love, and there never will be. Once you accept His love, you'll not need to seek it from others. You'll have enough to give to everyone around you."

As she spat out her words, the upper part of her body continued to sway, and the jerky movements of her head and the flashing of her angry eyes made her seem even more terrifying. Now she uncoiled and made quick sixes and eights around me, hissing as she went.

"Why were you making fun of that poor little duck-billed platypus? You're the one who can't make up your mind. You can't decide whether you want to be stone or human." A note of tolerance came into her voice for the first time, but it was still hard and demanding. "Accept your fear. All persons are afraid. Everyone has wanted love thousands of times. Such wanting has brought disappointment and pain more often than not. The pain remains permanently recorded in your brain, and cumulatively it results in fear so great that being hurt again becomes intolerable. That's how love became a meaningless word to you humans, and you've given up trying to feel the meaningful emotion. Grapple with your fears. Defeat their strangling hold so you can let go of all distrust. Then you can tap God's power line and be as forgetful of self as an electric wire."

Instantly terror gave way to awe. There appeared against a field of blackness huge gold transmission towers supporting thousands of golden wires. The nearest tower seemed to touch the dome of heaven, and others, each successively smaller, reached to the far horizon. Towers and wires alike twinkled continuously like millions of stars. Then surrounding each tower appeared great masses of humanity stretching their arms upward. A second later, myriads of golden wires fell from the mighty towers, transforming each into Maypoles of fantastic beauty. The reaching arms jerked back in terror.

Overwhelmed by both beauty and tragedy, I realized that the vision symbolized God's love and our own fear of accepting any type of genuine love. I understood more fully than ever before why so few people possessed outgoing warmth and why so many starved for affection.

Suddenly I was miserably cold, chills running through my stone-like body, my teeth chattering.

The cobra's long red tongue darted toward me unceasingly. "You're cold, are you? All the roaring fires in your fireplace, the thermostats and electric blankets turned high, the hot beverages, and heavy clothing will never warm you. There's only one source of warmth. That's love."

The chill became so exaggerated that it changed to actual pain. I called to Dr. Davidson, asking him to bring me hot bouillon, and telling him I was thirsty. I felt utterly miserable, crying loudly while I waited. In the same way that one can be relatively composed during an emergency but go to pieces afterward, the cobra's attack seemed even more blood-curdling during these moments of semiclarity than when her heinous face was near mine.

Dr. Davidson had scarcely closed the door after bringing the bouillon before the cobra was again hissing contemptuously. "If that cup held the Pacific Ocean, it could never quench your thirst. Your thirst is for love. That's why people drink too much. I have already told you, there's only one source of love."

Although the freezing terror continued, I suddenly felt starved. I had eaten nothing all day and little the evening before.

Quick as the darting of her malicious eyes, the cobra was prodding me again. "Your hunger can never be satisfied by food. Hunger for food is the only hunger you humans recognize. Millions of you eat too much, trying to satisfy a hunger which in reality is a hunger for love, a yearning for God. Once you accept love, or God Who is love, such hunger disappears."

Suddenly a total and terrifying blackness enveloped me. Quickly I pushed back the sleep shade, but the fading light of day could not pierce this darkness; the electric lights could not pierce it. Even the cobra was blotted out, but her voice, a combined shout and hiss, was appallingly close to my ear.

"Coward! Coward! You do everything you can to keep yourself from feeling, like concerning yourself with the history of India. Did Christ, Buddha, or Mohammed teach you people to clutter up your minds with things you can easily find in libraries and encyclopedias? They talked of a philosophy of love, direct in its simplicity. Your little conscious mind can hold only one thing at a time. If you choose a bit of worthless information, your feelings are crowded out. In your cowardly terror you choose information purposely. That's why your culture overemphasizes intellectual development. You use your gaining of knowledge as a defense against the very feelings you crave."

The unfathomable darkness seemed like a massive weight, crushing life out of me. With every attack, the cobra's venom appeared to become even more deadly, and I continued to cringe, still crying loudly.

"Coward! Coward!" she shrieked. "Why do you think you keep yourself busy, busy, busy, going about in turmoil fashion? Did the great seers teach a philosophy of being busy? Can't you remember that they talked of tranquillity and peace? It's fear of love which keeps you humans overbusy, which crowds out your peace and tranquillity. You purposely keep yourself too busy so that you can't feel your longings and thirsts and hungers."

Her silence was ominous as she made a few quick circles near me. Lurching the upper part of her body into the air, she attacked again with fresh ferocity.

"Christ, Buddha, and Mohammed also talked of life everlasting. You mouth such a belief on Sunday, you hypocrite, and the rest of the week you hurry. If you actually believed in eternity, you'd feel no need to hurry."

So great was the all-possessing terror that it was difficult to comprehend her words. In addition, the impenetrable blackness now seemed like a giant's spiked heel which completely covered me, grinding me with excruciating pain into nothingness. In horrified anguish, I lay gasping, yet crying even more loudly.

A period of clarity came, but it brought no relief. I took a few sips of the bouillon, lukewarm now and unappetizing. After a short time, I got shakily to my feet and put a small mountain of used facial tissues into a wastebasket, then took a fresh supply from the table near the davenport. The light seemed glaring; I switched off the lamp, leaving the room in a somewhat soothing darkness. This time I covered myself with two blankets.

Soon the cobra was at me again, her attack as vicious as before. "Why do you have a culture of things, things, things? All of you collect things like small boys collecting bugs and stones. Christ said, 'Lay not up for yourselves treasures upon earth, where moth and rust doth corrupt, and where thieves break through and steal.' He told you that where your treasure is, there will your heart be also. But you ignore His words, for when you can keep your mind on things, you don't have to feel your hungers and longings. Why do you think Christ said it was easier for a camel to pass through a needle's eye than for a rich man to enter the kingdom of heaven? The rich man's life is cluttered up with Cadillacs, yachts, stock-market reports, estates, and a thousand other things of little value. He has no time to feel. When a person once accepts God's love, he's too rich to be bothered with things. That's why men like Siddhartha, Tolstoi, and Gandhi gave up all they had."

I felt I could not endure her horrible hissing another instant. "I know I'm afraid of letting go," I managed to mumble between sobs, "but I think I can love, at least a little."

She struck at me with words as quickly as if by venom. "What is it you humans love? Your families, your friends, your dogs, your cats, your Swedish crystal, and all the hundreds of things with which you clutter your homes. You purposely disperse your love, using it as a defense against the truly great love which frightens you but which could fill your void."

She was gliding in circles around me as if she were considering what to say next. Then she recoiled.

"And how is it you love? If your children, husband, or friends displease you, I notice you withdraw your love quickly enough. Is love something you can jerk away at will? Real love is like the sun. It warms every heart within its radiance, not a selected few. Christ told you, 'He maketh his sun to rise on the evil and on the good, and sendeth rain on the just and on the unjust.' "

For a moment her head seemed to touch my ear, and I jerked back in still greater terror.

"What happens when you cannot love yourself? At least most of you humans are honest enough to say you dislike yourselves, but then you claim to love someone else. The two are incongruous, completely incompatible. You identify yourself with persons you love, as if they were editions of yourself. Because of this identification, it's impossible to love anyone until you can love yourself, totally and without egotism. You confuse the word need with love."

Despite the fact that I was freezing cold, rigid, seemingly paralyzed, and consumed with horror, I could still appreciate the wisdom of her words.

She uncoiled again, glided away a few feet, and returned to renew her hissing. "How is it you humans love in your marriages? 'I'll give you some love if you give me some.' Isn't that true? Is love something to be bartered, like cabbages in the market place? What you people call love is an infinitesimal fraction of what Christ, Buddha, and Mohammed talked about."

"I've prayed for greater love," I cried in despair.

"Yes, and I've heard your prayers. Gimme, gimme, gimme, like a kid begging for candy, with a few words of thanks in trade for expected sweets. Even in your prayers you can't let yourself go. Try to be like an open vessel so that God may fill your emptiness."

It seemed that I could not tolerate the terror a moment longer. "Please help me," I pleaded. "I'll admit I'm afraid, but I'm less frightened in your skin than in mine. May I borrow it again?"

I had scarcely finished speaking when every muscle shook as if it were in the grip of a torturous convulsion. A new terror caused goose pimples to rise over my entire body. I had the feeling that my hair was standing on end and that the cobra, angered by my request, had finally struck me. This time I screamed in sheer horror.

An eternity seemed to pass before I realized that the snake was merely shedding her old skin to give me a new one. The instant this awareness came, the dark room was saturated with sunshine, and a marvelous security flooded me from head to toe. Again I was the cobra, this time with a more brilliantly beautiful skin than before. Although I no longer saw the cobra who had given me her skin, I knew she was beside me, her presence reassuring now instead of frightening.

Quietly Dr. Davidson opened the door and walked noiselessly across the room, taking the chair beside the davenport. I blessed him for not asking the cause of my screaming and loud crying. Indeed his very silence made me welcome his presence. With the coming of the sunshine, love had flowed into me, and I directed its course to him. Soon I heard the cobra's voice say softly. "Follow me."

We stopped on a grassy knoll beside a tranquil river where we were caressed by warm breezes. Quietly the water lapped against the bank and rippled and murmured as it flowed past large rocks covered with green moss. At the far side of the stream great overhanging willows were reflected in mirror-clear stillness. The whispering of birds, the fluttering of insect wings, and the soft songs of leaves blended into gentleness. Peace and love seemed to open doors into every cell of my body, filling me to overflowing.

After a few moments of blissful ecstasy, terror struck again, seemingly without cause. Only later did I realize that the reason was my deep fear of yielding completely and selflessly to love. "I've taken sunbaths for years," I exclaimed nonchalantly, moving rapidly through a lacework of ferns. Soon I added more seriously, "Each of us must grow in his own way. Mine can't be yours." Quickly I slithered on, going I knew not where.

Next I was aware of being surrounded by a shimmering landscape with moonlight rimming great clouds with gold. This time I was lying under the bodhi tree where Buddha had seen his visions. I recalled that Buddha had said, "Be kind to those cruel to you and love your enemies," then thinking that no person was cruel unless someone had first been cruel to him; that if you gave him kindness and love, he would cease being cruel; and that when you could love your enemies, they would no longer be enemies. Again I marveled at how amazingly Christ's teachings resembled those of Buddha and Mohammed.

While lying leisurely under the bodhi tree, a delicious harmony covered me like a blanket, seeping into every pore. Something told me it existed in everything in the universe: in our world, on other planets, and throughout the cosmos; only our own warped feelings and our tragically myopic vision kept us from recognizing this harmony; and it had existed since time began and would exist throughout all eternity. As tranquillity amounted to euphoria, I thought, "This is the way a person should feel when he's dying." Then I realized that my problem was to learn how to live—and truly love—not how to die.

I became aware that Dr. Davidson had started the music and that a Bach *Prelude* was being played. Its familiar strains seemed far more beautiful than ever before, yet sorrowful and disconsolate. A streak of light coming from under a door gave the room a somber, eerie quality, deepening my depression still more. While I was in this mood, the drug again possessed me.

"How can one learn to quiet fears enough to love selflessly?" I asked, feeling filled with despair. Sadly I went on my way.

Still as a cobra, I next found myself with Christ in the Garden of Gethsemane. Slowly I followed His weary steps through the olive groves, passing over dry, hard clods and sharp rocks. The moon, too weak to give light, had hidden behind clouds; yet I knew the Master's feet were bleeding, and the skin on my belly was torn. I wondered why anyone had ever called this place a garden. We were not alone; beside us walked discouragement, loneliness, sadness, and desolation.

As Christ fell to the ground and prayed, I bowed my head and wept with an all-inclusive sorrow which seemed to encompass the sorrow of the entire world. "O my Father, if it be possible, let this cup pass from me . . ." I knew then that He, the human Jesus, was afraid, just as all of us have been afraid; if He feared not, He would not have uttered these words. His troubled voice came again: "Not my will, but thine, be done." The thought flashed through my mind of how often many of us have repeated His prayer, though giving it our own meaning: "Thy will be done as long as Thy will agrees with my will." Then Christ rose and went back to His disciples, and I felt sure He knew even then that He must face the shamefully cruel death upon the cross. As He walked, I saw in Him the embodiment of courage, that wonderful quality which allows us to go on when consumed with fear. Feeling overcome with gratitude, I cried aloud, knowing that Christ, by His death, had given each of us the courage to live.

A great reverence settled over me; simultaneously the room was transformed into a cathedral with beautiful stained-glass windows. It was then that I knew I must start afresh, and I gave myself rebirth by quickly shedding the cobra's skin. Immediately before me appeared Christ clad in soft robes of pale blue, a warm, golden radiance surrounding his entire body. Compassion showed in every line of His kind face, and in His arms He held with magnificent tenderness a baby lamb of the purest white. I became that lamb and felt His gentle arms supporting me, and I experienced, as a living, throbbing joy, His love and tenderness as it flowed into me.

Next I was a filthy beggar child, starved, weak, and clothed in rags, standing on tiptoe in the midst of a crowd and hoping to get a glimpse of Jesus. Someone was yelling, "Go away! Go away!" Cuffs and kicks with which I was all too familiar fell on my legs, arms, and buttocks, quick, sharp pains cutting into me. Then I heard Christ say, "Suffer little children to come unto me, and forbid them not: for of such is the kingdom of God." The crowd made way, and I walked to Him. He laid His hand on my head, and immediately I was beautiful and clean and dressed in a spotless tunic; yet the beauty which He put in my heart was far greater than beauty which eyes can see.

Suddenly I felt ill to the point of death, so weak that it seemed impossible to move. I could see a large crowd gathered around a small flat-roofed building, every person listening intently, and I knew Christ was talking. Friends who wished to reach Jesus were carrying me on a litter, for I was paralyzed and had lost all hope. When the crowd would not let us through, my friends approached the building from the rear, removed part of a wooden roof, and lowered me with much jostling to the ground inside. Christ bent over me and, with a gentle smile on His face, said, "Rise, take up thy bed, and walk." Although I had not taken a step in years and could scarcely lift my hand, a tremendous strength flooded into me. Filled with joy and marveling at the wonder of it, I picked up the litter and passed through the door it had been impossible to enter.

Then I was a harlot, used by many and shunned by all, the shame and ostracism which was my lot pressing hard against me. I had heard that Jesus was near and I wanted desperately to see Him. As He walked through the village where I lived, I furtively skirted a large group of His followers. Again and again persons turned to stone me, yelling curses. I lay weeping, feeling the utter defeat with which my life had been filled. Then Jesus heard, turned, and walked toward me, saying, "Go, and sin no more." His forgiveness caused my great load of shame to disappear. Such thankfulness surged through me that, thereafter, I tried to live as Christ had shown us how to live.

As my brain cleared, it seemed to me that all the emotions I had felt during the latter part of the afternoon had been much too intense to be expressed in words; yet the most overwhelming were those which I had just experienced. I could still feel the misery and joy of the beggar child, the shame and thankfulness of the harlot, the weakness and strength of the paralytic, and the love which filled me when Christ held me, a lamb, in His arms. It occurred to me that Christ must have been referring to love when He said, "But whosoever drinketh of the water that I shall give him shall never thirst"; and that He was speaking of a selfless acceptance of love when He continued, "but the water that I shall give him shall be in him a well of water springing up into everlasting life." I was thinking that there was surely no more beautiful passage in the entire Bible when I drifted back under the drug.

Next I was a blind man, blind to Christ's love and to every person's need for God. Christ came to me and took my hand and twice He laid His fingertips on my eyelids. Love and warmth flowed from His hand into me, and understanding and insight streamed from His fingertips into me, and I knew the meaning of things I had never comprehended before. Thus was my blindness cured.

A little later I saw before me a low mountain overlooking the plains of Syria. Shepherds were herding their flocks on its slopes. Near the summit, Christ stood with His disciples gathered around Him. As He spoke, I listened as intently as did they. "Blessed are the poor in spirit: for theirs is the kingdom of heaven." The meaning suddenly became obvious for the first time. The sad, depressed, and despondent would, in their misery, seek God; urged on by the sorrow within themselves, they would continue seeking Him until their lives were indeed made rich and their souls filled with joy; thus would theirs be the kingdom of heaven within, where Christ had repeatedly told us it would be found.

Now He was saying, "Blessed are the meek: for they shall inherit the earth." I realized that He was not referring to milksops or self-imposed martyrs or masochists, but that the only way one could be truly meek was by first accepting himself as a marvelous part of God. Once the God self was recognized and appreciated, all need for arrogance and egotism was gone. It was the necessary acceptance of our God selves which allowed both meekness and inheritance of the earth, meaning the inheritance of the kingdom of heaven within ourselves while we are still on this earth.

As Christ continued speaking, I realized that in one way or another we were all blessed and many times blessed, and that if we failed to recognize our blessedness, the problem lay in ourselves. When I looked up again, Christ was saying, "Ye are the salt of the earth. . . . Ye are the light of the world." It seemed to me Christ was saying that a part of God was in each of us.

The door opened, and Frank came in. Since his own LSD experience had been a deeply religious one, he sensed immediately that this was no time for talking. I said a half-whispered good-by to Dr. Davidson, and we left the room as quietly as if it were still the great cathedral I had seen perhaps an hour earlier.

During most of the trip home, I remained silent, the feeling of reverence within me still all-pervading. I felt great love for Frank and was deeply grateful to him for his understanding. Although we stopped at a drive-in and dinner trays were brought, mine was taken away untouched.

As soon as we reached home, I went directly to bed and quickly turned off the light. Almost immediately I was deep under the drug again. I found myself standing with a multitude, and we were listening intently as Christ talked. We had been thus all day, without shade or water or food, but it made no difference. Just to see and hear Him filled us with joy. Foolishly Christ's disciples became worried because they had only two fishes and five loaves to offer us, but we were not hungry for fish and bread. We were hungry for love, and with His love, Christ fed us. Later I heard the feast that day spoken of as a miracle, but I disagreed; I knew that anyone who accepts love can feed a multitude.

Suddenly I was in pitch blackness. My hands groped along

walls of rough dirt, and I ran down one dark passageway after another, led by the odor of a burning candle. The path was familiar, and it was easy to get bearings by the new graves set into the walls. As a Christian martyr, I was living among the dead in the catacombs. We gathered in small groups, talked in hushed voices, and listened to the news brought by friends who lived outside. Caesar could not prevent their coming; everyone had the right to visit graves.

Almost every night I slipped out to teach groups of people about Christ. For a time I sat crouched in a corner of a bare and dimly lighted room, telling a dozen or so persons about His miracles. As I left, Roman soldiers grabbed me and bound me with ropes which cut into my arms. In pain and terror, I was driven before them to a filthy prison.

When the next vision came, I could feel ropes being loosened. Kicks which felled me to the ground quickly followed. As I got up, I heard shouting and for an instant I saw the filled Colosseum, gay with brightly colored togas. Then electrifying terror gripped my entire body. Eight or ten lions, crazed with hunger to assure the jaded crowd a thrill, were preparing to attack me. I barely had time to raise my head proudly; I would not allow any person to see me cringe before my Saviour. Then I heard the tearing of my own flesh and knew pain excruciating beyond endurance. Soon came the blessed relief of death.

For a time I was St. Paul, preaching in Greece and being driven out of city after city and from many of the surrounding islands. Yet nothing could stop my compulsion to tell people of Christ and His teachings and of God. Again and again I was thrown into prison, but I was allowed to write letters to my friends and in them I recorded much of His life. In Rome I was arrested and appealed to Caesar. As I awaited freedom hopefully, I wrote still more letters. Next there appeared a clear vision of the great yellow basilica which is said to stand on the spot where I was killed. Sunshine sparkled so brightly on its beautiful windows of yellow and white marble that I knew my life had not been lived in vain.

Once more as myself or perhaps as a symbol of all humanity, I at last knew that God had indeed given me courage. I kept thinking of His words: "Enter ye in at the strait gate: for wide is the gate, and broad is the way, that leadeth to destruction, and many there be which go in thereat. Because strait is the gate, and narrow is the way, which leadeth unto life, and few there be that find it."

I repeated the Biblical quotation over and over, trying to understand its real meaning. Eventually it seemed to me that, to find the narrow way leading to life, one must become capable of selfless love; and that each of us had to face the problem of letting go of all distrust alone, provided we had the courage to face it at all. In the end, Christ, St. Paul, and the Christian martyrs each had been alone.

The final vision showed a broad landscape, flat from horizon to horizon. Dawn was beginning to break, and though there was darkness overhead and the birds were still hushed, the eastern sky was pale yellow splashed with delicate pink. Against this background of light I watched myself in black silhouette walk toward the rising sun. Although God's courage was in my footsteps, the fear in my heart caused me to repeat with each breath what seemed to me to be the password to the strait gate, "Alone, alone, alone."

As I walked, massive swirls of sparkling golden mists crept softly over the entire sky. Then from one great cloud came His voice, "Alone? I shall be with you always, even unto the end."

CHAPTER 10

An Experience in Selfless Love

IT HAD become obvious that the content of LSD visions could be influenced by my thoughts and feelings immediately preceding the experience; hence I prepared for my fifth session like a theological student cramming for an examination.

A week earlier, when I had given a report to Dr. Davidson, he had remarked, "You haven't had any mystical experiences yet."

I was amazed, aware that mystical was synonymous with religious, though why it should be when its root was the same as mysterious and mystery had always puzzled me; I had had far more religious feelings and insights during four days under the drug than in hundreds of Sundays of church attendance.

Since I had taken LSD in the hope of spiritual enrichment but had apparently not reached its potentialities, I spent considerable time during the following week reading the Bible. On Sunday, we went to church, and the night before the experience I attended Latihan, religious exercises directed at reaching the God elements inside ourselves. Before going to bed, I read a small book on religious meditation and completed my efforts with prayers, followed by ten hours of sleep. Probably as a result, I encountered only a few moments of terror when on February 23, 1960, Dr. Janiger gave me 150 micrograms of the drug. On the whole, I was unusually calm.

Perhaps half an hour after Dr. Davidson had made me comfortable on the davenport, covered me with a blanket, and handed me the sleep shade, I noticed that the familiar *Second Symphony* of Brahms then being played had taken on exaggerated and overwhelming beauty. Soon the music seemed to lift me with infinite tenderness into the air where I floated bodiless and weightless, moving gently in rhythm and rising and falling with each crescendo and diminuendo.

Although I was aware of breathing deeply and yawning repeatedly, the marvelous feelings of being weightless, boneless, and bodiless persisted throughout most of the day. At all times I was as free from the fear of falling as would be a bit of thistledown. Being cushioned on air and caressed by the arms of space caused glorious sensations amounting to ecstasy. Other strong emotions quickly increased my feelings to euphoria: a tremendously deep love seemingly for every person and thing in the world, including love for myself untainted by egotism; a peaceful, all-pervading reverence which came from the feeling that God existed in all things; and, despite a conviction that I had happily ceased to exist, an amazingly intense feeling of aliveness. During the entire experience, I felt I had no more need of a body than has the odor of jasmine for a flower, once its fragrance rides the mists of night. As in previous experiences, emotions came in rip tides, thoughts poured out in torrents, and my entire body moved almost continuously, its actions prompted by the content of the visions.

Soon I realized I was a speck of dust floating leisurely and luxuriously in a brilliant shaft of sunlight, sparkling as if made of the richest gold. Because I was gold, I knew I was part of God. Because I was part of God, I was joyous to be nothing but dust. The feeling of reverence became still more overpowering as the words, "For dust thou art, and unto dust shalt thou return," lost all fatalistic meaning, and something told me this golden bit of dust was in reality my soul which would live on forever. Such gladness filled me that it swiftly increased to ecstasy and as rapidly changed to the severe pain of intense joy. I cried aloud, writhing in agony, a crying and writhing which scarcely stopped during the next nine hours.

Vividly I relived a specific incident when as a child I had been fascinated by bits of dust dancing in afternoon sunlight in my aunt's dining room. The cool, comfortable room, the shaft of sunlight, and the golden dust appeared with realistic clarity before me. The shades were pulled against the summer's heat. I could hear the lazy buzzing of flies and an occasional low cackle of a hen and a far-off mooing of a cow. Then all was silent. Peace filled my world, a peace which in its will-o'-the-wispness had seemed to evade me since childhood. Now peace again entered my soul, and I felt, crying out in gratitude, that this time it had come to stay. My emotions became so overwhelming that they cannot be put into words.

As a speck of dust yet overpowered with feelings of aliveness, reverence, and love for all mankind, I next floated in a shaft of sunlight coming through a small window in a tiny village church in Mexico. With tender affection I watched a woman dressed and veiled in black praying at a poor altar. Still as a bit of dust, a second later I was in the center of the great Greek Orthodox Cathedral of Saint Sophia, given by Spyros Skouras to the Greek people of Los Angeles, surely one of the most beautiful churches in the world. At the elaborate altar, priests swinging incense pots wore white robes heavily embroidered with gold. The massive chandeliers glistened their beauty, the choir caroled praises to God, and the congregation below me knelt in prayer. Great shafts of sunlight came through each of the superb windows which showed Biblical characters pictured in glass of rich blues, brilliant reds, royal purples, and soft golds. These shafts of light miraculously converged upon me, carrying with them the bright colors of the glass. Yet they could not change my gold-of-God loveliness. As I watched, it came to me that the smallest church was as great as the most magnificent cathedral and that wherever man prayed, there was his church and his God also.

Soon I was floating in the silence of yet another shaft of sunlight, this time in a forest of giant redwoods. With eyes still filled with reverence and love, I could see God's strength in the dignity of the trees, God's glory in the blueness of the sky, and God's beauty in the lush greenness of the fern-covered ground. God's peace was in the whole, pervading alike trees, sky, ferns, and my soul, bringing both joy and sadness so great that tears could not be held back.

Next my field of vision was filled with a vast landscape. Below me were towering peaks and beautiful valleys which symbolized the strengths and weaknesses in us all. Milling about in torment were massive clouds of rich purples, deep blues, and angry grays, representing both the rewards and struggles of life. The clouds separated slightly and allowed a great shaft of sheer gold sunlight to come through and fan out to flood the earth. This time I was swallowed up in radiance and, as a joyous nothing, felt I was face to face with my Creator. As my entire body shook with sobs, I knew the reason we could not see God: His brilliance was too blinding.

Dr. Davidson, who had been sitting near the davenport but slightly behind me, got up to change records. I pushed back the sleep shade and watched him select the music which he thought would be most satisfying to me. Even a few moments without music now seemed a severe deprivation. Throughout this experience the lovely symphonies seemed to be inside me and a part of me. Never before had I been so aware of every component of sound or the magnificence of the whole. As visions shifted continuously with breath-taking speed and thoughts pelted my brain, the music constantly filled me with a sort of exploding force impossible to describe. At the same time it was the stabilizing influence which maintained my sanity as wave after wave of soul-shattering emotions engulfed me.

Next I became the spirit of music, another aspect of God and my soul which filled me anew with reverence and all-encompassing love. I danced weightlessly in midair while before me appeared a hundred or more visions: symphony orchestras playing in bowls and concert halls; nude African natives beating strange-shaped drums in small clearings in dense jungles; congregations singing hymns in churches large and small; warm-hearted Hawaiians leisurely strumming ukuleles; devout monks chanting in the predawn darkness of chilled chapels; West Indian Negroes shaking gourds and joyously clanging tops of carefully reshaped oil drums; a great choir praising God with the *Hallelujah Chorus;* family groups gathered around living-room pianos; muffled and mittened children caroling Christmas joys; cowpunchers, boy- and girl-scout troops, and camping parties of many varieties encircling bonfires; and lastly an orchestra of crickets amid wildernesses of stems of grasses, grains, and weeds, singing through lazy afternoons, balmy twilights, and star-filled nights. With each vision I heard exquisite music. Familiar symphonies, songs, and hymns, far surpassing their actual beauty, were intermingled with magnificent music which my brain composed with amazing spontaneity.

As I watched these visions, it occurred to me that the importance of music was, like art, its power to convey emotions we were too hurt, too timid, or too inarticulate to express directly: love, compassion, sweetness, tenderness, warmth, loneliness, sadness, despair, discouragement, and the gamut of pains and joys. It seemed to me that music was great only in so far as it could catch and interpret these universal feelings. In a language surmounting all boundaries and race barriers, music spoke alike to young and old, sick and healthy, sane and insane. I thought of how the yearnings of many composers had reached, where words could not, into the souls of the insane, withdrawn in their oppressive aloneness, and assured them they were not alone.

The curtain fell, but the music still seemed to clutch at every atom of my body, and for several minutes I lay sobbing softly, not wanting to speak or lift the sleep shade. Dr. Davidson too remained silent. Soon the feeling came again of rising and falling with each crescendo and diminuendo, the latter quickly taking over as I became a series of falling objects, all of which seemed again to be manifestations of God.

First I was a small rock being carried in Galileo's dark and dirty pocket up the winding steps inside the tower of Pisa; he dropped me together with a larger rock. As I neared the ground, I could see two oddly dressed men squatting and watching to determine which of us fell the more rapidly, and then heard them exclaim that both of us had landed at exactly the same time.

Next I became the falling blossoms of many varieties of

flowering trees, forming carpets of fragrant pastels; the petals of gay, brilliantly colored flowers dropping on shaded earth in gardens, meadows, and pastures; the winged seeds of soft maples; ripened plums, pears, peaches, and apples falling on orchard floors thick with grass; the fluff of dandelion and milkweed pod soaring in freedom across late summer landscapes before reaching the ground; thistledown gracefully carried over harvested fields and fence-row hedges of orange-red bittersweet as I hunted and found a brown winter bed. I became leaves of every intensity of red, yellow, orange, and brown, falling from glorious forests, making way for the restless beginnings of new spring growth; yellow-brown grasses and dry, pithy weedstalks bowing as if in prayer to the winter snows; and lastly huge pine cones dropping from majestic trees on mountain slopes and landing almost noiselessly on years-old beds of soft, brown needles.

In each case the sensation of falling was similar to that of soaring and was accompanied by such great delight that it became ecstasy; yet the feelings of aliveness, reverence, and love remained uppermost. The sum total of all these emotions seemed to blend into the music, and soon the whole changed to pain, renewing my sobs.

Again I was back in reality. This time I raised the sleep shade and looked around the attractively furnished room which had taken on new meaning for me with each experience. It now seemed like a home that I had gradually learned to love. I also felt a great warmth for Dr. Davidson and was equally grateful for his presence and his silence.

Soon I became a drop of water bubbling with carefree abandon from an underground spring in the Colorado mountains. Reverently I valued the feeling that God possessed this water droplet which somehow symbolized my soul and yet was myself. Around me I could see meadows of grazing land

and towering peaks which pierced an intensely blue sky dotted with majestic clouds of bluish whiteness. A cowboy, lying prone, took me into his mouth, gave me a moment's terror as he jostled me between tongue and teeth; since his mouth was dry, he spat me out. I quickly slid downhill, eagerly joined other drops of water, and together we worked our way around bits of bark, stones, and grass stems to a small brook. The stream, bordered by willows, grew steadily larger; soon mountain trout with spotted bellies were darting past us. At times I was caught in pools near the bank, gradually gathered force with the current and, like a sprinter, eddied quickly around tufts of grass. In laughing rapids we danced gaily and joyously, passed through groves of aspen sheltering log cabins, and floated on, viewing constantly changing scenes, the sky half-hidden by a lacework of overhanging willows.

For a winter we rested quietly in the peace of a beaver dam, watching by moonlight as beavers made wedge-shaped cuts in trees, felled them, and with supernatural strength, pulled them to the dam. The rhythmical chip, chip, chip of cutting teeth, the pat, pat, pat of flat tails on soft mud, and the continuous trickle of the stream lulled me with a sense of all-pervading peace. Through an opalescent layer of ice we watched skiers slalom past snow-bowed trees and come to abrupt halts beside the stream, their bright clothing making gay patterns against sparkling whiteness. With the spring thaws, we were washed on and went laughing, splashing, dancing, leaping, floating, eddying, and whirling through great canyons, and passed overhanging cliffs and tranquil new-green meadows. Tiny spotted fawns came with does to drink while I looked into their huge eyes seemingly filled with trust. Joyously we made our way through many rapids and on into the Gunnison River where we tossed and roared down the rugged Black Canyon, mountains pressing close against us.

As in the last of the first experience and the beginning of the third, the scenes already viewed and those to follow, though commonplacc enough, were nature in exaggerated excellence, vividly clear, aglitter, and lovely. Thus was I made so continuously aware of the many aspects of God that the feelings of love and reverence were ever present.

Eventually I, as a drop of water, reached the sea, evaporated, and was carried north in a cloud. As a snowflake I fell on the summit of Mount Rainier. Below me in every direction seemed endless mountain ranges whose beauty, especially at sunrise and sunset, was too breath-taking for camera to catch. Through violent blizzards, jeweled mists, blue-cold nights, and sparkling sunshine, I watched from one spot as scenes changed constantly, seeming to vie with each other for magnificence. With summer heat, I made my way past glaciers, in and out of blue ice caves, over ground covered with brightly colored wild flowers, and through pine forests where bears ambled lazily toward me.

In similar manner I fell on farmland in Indiana, moistened the roots of growing corn, watched a farm girl land a catfish, and traveled the Wabash, Ohio, and Mississippi Rivers into the Gulf, a thousand scenes passing before my eyes. After floating around cypress trees and watching crabs and shrimp in a Louisiana bayou, I was carried to sea and via the Gulf Stream toward Greenland, where I saw blue, green, and yellow lights play on glistening icebergs.

Next I fell as rain on mountains high above the Norwegian fjords, my vision encompassing beauty in rugged cliffs, waterfalls, winding waterways, and homes precariously perched on 45-degree slopes which served as farms. I joined a stream, and from tremendous heights we splashed in ecstasy into a fjord. After diving deep into freezing black water, I surfaced to enjoy, by looking upward this time, ever-changing views of majestic beauty.

The combined emotions were so overpowering that it was almost a relief when the wave passed. Dr. Davidson helped me to my feet, and I walked unsteadily to the office where Eve told me it was already one o'clock. For a few moments I gazed out a window, thinking that the clear, bright day was colorless and drab. Weakness came over me, and I returned and lay down again on the davenport, Dr. Davidson quickly taking his chair to my right.

Soon I was falling as gentle raindrops or soft snowflakes on many lands in many seasons, traveling the earth more completely than Thomas Cook could have planned. At one point I shot the rapids of the Colorado River and reviewed the beauty of the Grand Canyon. Another time I fell with euphoric abandon down both the two roaring waterfalls of Yellowstone and a half dozen or more falls in Yosemite Valley, feeling as a child must who discovers a high slide for the first time and does not want to stop sliding.

Finally I dropped on a pine forest in northern Minnesota. In much the same way as an opera singer aspires to reach the Metropolitan or La Scala, it seemed to me that the ambition of every raindrop was to plunge over Niagara Falls. Quickly I made my way into Lake Superior, then impatiently and with tremendous difficulty, tried to force myself on through currentless water. Years passed before I neared the falls. With ever-mounting excitement, I swirled faster and faster, the roar of the falls at last becoming audible. As the rumble became increasingly louder, I was tossed high into the air, sucked into whirlpools, swung to dizziness in eddies, spun in vortexes of varying sizes, and plunged with terrific force against rocks, overcome with a multiplicity of emotions while my body went through as many antics as a bucking bronco.

Despite the violence of the tumbling, falling, leaping, spraying, and splashing, I was experiencing a form of divine ecstasy. It seemed to me that a God force, a God strength, existed not only inside me and in everything around me but was being demonstrated to me in such a way that it could never be forgotten. His force or strength increased with each moment I was shaken to giddiness, dropped onto soft cushions of foam, blinded by splashing water, and whirled to dizzy madness. Then as the roar became deafening. I was over the rim, falling with wings of freedom and love into an epitome of euphoria, all chains broken, all fetters gone. For what seemed half an hour, I was spinning, whirling, twirling, twisting down, down, down into an infinity of bliss, crying aloud with emotions so overpowering as to become torturous.

I threw my right hand over my head, and Dr. Davidson took it warmly in both of his, making it possible for me to endure depths of feelings I believe no person could experience alone. Although he remained consistently his own sweet self, he instantly became a composite of several men who had meant much in my life: my father, who had been a Gibraltar of stability; Frank, my beloved husband; and the analyst and psychotherapist who had each accepted me through many hundred hours of tears and joys.

Gradually I became aware of being back in the prison of my body. The tumble through the seeming infinity of space had been so violent and soul shaking that I felt emotionally exhausted. I lay thinking how the feelings accompanying the dust particle, the music spirit, each falling object, and the adventures of the drop of water had all been deeply religious ones in which I had been a part of God. All the beauty I had seen had likewise been a part of God. The conviction grew stronger that every person who lives or had lived was a part of God and would continue to be throughout all eternity. This recognition of the immortality of the divine in ourselves was not an intellectual process but rather a deep wisdom which had expressed itself through feelings so intense I expect to remember them throughout life.

At that moment I was much too overcome with my immediate emotions to give a thought to their interpretation. Understanding came weeks later when I realized that the spirit of music and the many inanimate objects I had believed myself to be were symbols which had made it possible for me to experience love with complete forgetfulness of self; that I had actually felt the selfless love I had feared during the fourth LSD session; and that the feelings of intense aliveness were in reality a keen awareness of my overwhelming love for all who live. The conviction that I no longer existed, which was indeed selflessness, I had already experienced many times but had failed to recognize as such; hence it was presented repeatedly in increasingly forceful forms. At last I realized that only after I could forget myself enough to be carried away with love was I ready for a profound mystical experience.

Such thoughts, however, were now far from my mind. I still lay sobbing quietly, pressing Dr. Davidson's hand and loving him as a representative of all humanity.

CHAPTER 11

The Caverns of the Soul

THE FIFTH experience was passing as rapidly as the others, but the accompanying emotions had already been so rich and fulfilling that I felt no regret.

When my crying subsided, Dr. Davidson asked, "Do you wish to tell me what's been happening?"

I gave him a quick synopsis, mentioning that as a drop of water I had seeped underground.

"When you're below the surface, never hurry to get out," he advised.

Immediately I was part of a small pool swirling in darkness and carrying away a tiny sharp stone, a single grain of sand, a bit of clay, then dropping them and tirelessly picking up other loads. As drops of water we worked with infinite patience throughout all the billions of years it has taken the soul of man to evolve. In this manner we formed huge caverns which symbolized the various aspects of the soul, that part of each of us which is also a part of God.

A conviction arrived at during the first experience now returned in even greater force: that among other things the soul was the sum total of our feelings. It seemed to me that the soul uses the nervous system and brain much as a plane uses a landing strip and hangar; and that at death, like a plane zooming from a runway, it soared unhampered into the ether. The soul no longer needed a body any more than did air-borne notes of a song need a throat. I felt that one purpose of earthly existence was to develop all our positive feelings and particularly our love for God, thereby increasing the depth and richness of the soul; and that if these feelings were allowed to live now, they would continue to live throughout all eternity. Such convictions made themselves known in a thousandth of the time it takes to write them; yet they had instantly become deeply rooted.

As a drop of water, I had scarcely finished helping prepare the caverns of the soul when I trickled into a vast cave. Glowing emeralds, rubies, topazes, garnets, amethysts, and sapphires formed irregular walls, floor, and ceiling of fantastic beauty. The massive stones, most of them several feet in diameter and all lit from within, had rounded water-worn edges and were polished as only the great Lapidary could polish them. The light which shone from within the huge gems gave the entire room a soft, warm radiance, each rich color blending harmoniously with the next. This cavern symbolized the true worth of man, the God self within every human being. As I watched, there swept over me feelings of reverence and spirituality of such magnitude that all else was blotted out. Soon came a deep gratitude for the privilege of seeing this divine part of myself and others.

Instead of my emotions subsiding after the plunge over Niagara, they had actually increased until it seemed that surely no person had ever experienced such feelings. God was beside me; yet His strength and His love were within me. Now my emotions grew even more intense; tiny particles of the gems from the cavern were forming three radiant multicolored columns of swirling mists. These glistening round columns, symbolizing beauty, pain, and music, stood side by side. As they slowly elongated upward, the light of God, soft, yet of inexpressible splendor, played upon them. The mists continuously intermingled, pain blending with beauty, music with pain, and beauty with music. Although the columns rose steadily and majestically and the mists continued their ceaseless swirling and intermingling, they never lost their identity. The soft yet brilliant light caused the jewel fragments to glisten with indescribable loveliness. When the whole had reached the dome of heaven, the three rounded columns twisted together into a great pillar many yards wide. It took a place at the extreme left of a night sky, its base standing in midair at about the height of a high hill. There it remained sparkling, twinkling, and brilliant, yet inconceivably fragile, to be seen more than a dozen times later.

The columns, mists, and pillar had each somehow symbolized God. The exquisite blending of beauty, pain, and music, and the overpowering awareness of the presence of God made me feel worshipful, overcome with reverence, and bursting with love. The combined emotions left me writhing in a flood of joy-to-agony tears. I believe that only the pressure of Dr. Davidson's hand and the beauty of the symphony then being played saved my sanity.

After the vision had disappeared, the words of a Chinese philosopher rang in my mind: "He who knows does not say; and he who says does not know." The statement seemed to summarize the impossibility of describing what I had just seen and felt. Now I understood as never before that he who knows does not say because he cannot say and that he who says does not know that he does not know.

The emotions I had just felt were as exaggerated in comparison with previous drug-induced feelings as these latter emotions were with those of everyday life. They towered to mountain heights, plunged to oceanic depths, soared on wings of air, or rolled like vast, restless clouds, even at times grinding me to pulp as if massive wheels were passing over me. I did not know that all emotions I was to experience during the afternoon would be equally violent.

I turned to Dr. Davidson, exclaiming, "The colossal egotism of anyone who thinks he can write an LSD report! It can't be done, not with all the languages in the world!"

"No one can tell an experience," he replied. "An experience has to be experienced."

Korzybski had pointed out that our deepest feelings exist only on what he had spoken of as "the silent, unspeakable level," I remembered, feeling sure that I would always hold this experience guardedly to myself and that anything else would be sacrilege. Still, I had promised to write a report.

These thoughts were abruptly terminated by my again becoming a drop of water trickling in underground darkness. Soon I passed into another huge chamber of such unutterable beauty that I first caught my breath, then cried aloud, sobbing continuously until the wave passed. In this cavern lights of every pastel shade played on smooth walls and majestic stalactites and stalagmites. As magnificent music rose to crescendos and dropped to diminuendos, the lights became more brilliant or delicate, all joyously dancing with exquisite grace. I knew this cavern was a hall of art, symbolizing another part of God which lies in the soul of every human being, whether recognized or not.

Again there formed before me three columns of multicolored mists which seemed infinitely soft and yet glowed as if set with all the world's gems, each tiny, glistening jewel lit from within. I lifted my hands slowly higher and higher, gesturing with the intertwining of beauty, pain, and music until another pillar of God had formed. This one took its place at my extreme right, far across a vast sky of warm darkness from the other. Now a pillar glowed on either side, the one last viewed seeming the more glorious. Again I was engulfed with a love so magnanimous and reverence so profound that it was almost beyond enduring, and I quickly dropped my hands and reached for Dr. Davidson's, blessing him for his comfort while I sobbed.

As if it were necessary for the maintenance of sanity, I returned to reality and lay emotionally exhausted, the profound feelings of love and reverence still hanging over me like a cloud. Again I realized that such feelings could never be adequately described. Furthermore this experience was about my very soul, the most sacred part of any person. Then I remembered that I had been tremendously curious to know what a mystical experience was and had been repeatedly disappointed when persons having had such experiences while under LSD invariably remained silent. Why should one be ashamed to bare one's soul? The soul of one person is probably much like that of another. Then I realized, thinking of Eleanor, that it was not shame which kept persons silent but the sheer impossibility of communication.

Only a few months earlier Eleanor had had several drug experiences which I had been more than eager to hear about. When we were at last face to face across a restaurant table, I opened the subject immediately by remarking, "I'm dying to hear what happened."

"I've been dying to tell you, but there's one little fly in the ointment. It's untellable."

I had no idea what she meant, but her high color, quick breathing, and the expression on her face showed she was overcome with emotion.

"What did you see?" I persisted.

"I saw God."

"But what was it you actually saw?"

"I really didn't see anything, but I felt His presence. It was so overpowering it forced you to love everyone. In fact, it was impossible not to love everyone, even for weeks afterward."

That was all I learned, and I had remained puzzled until now when I too felt God's overwhelming love. It became clear for the first time why stirring spiritual experiences were spoken of as mystical: one can describe actions, surroundings, and happenings in such a way that they can be comprehended, but deep emotions can be understood only after they have been felt. I knew that, since it was impossible to communicate them, they must forever remain mysterious, an unsolved mystery to all who have not had such feelings. If any person would recall the most intensely religious emotions he had ever experienced and then try to imagine multiplying them a hundredfold to allow for LSD magnification, it seemed to me that he would understand the impossibility of putting such feelings into words. It occurred to me that almost nothing had been told of Christ's mystical experience in the desert, and that Buddha's enlightenment was said to have been incommunicable.

There came a feeling of floating in rapidly moving water as the drug again took possession of me. This time I swirled into a cavern of phosphorescent stones which glowed with warm yet striking brilliance. Many smaller chambers opened from the main one, partly concealed by the many narrow columns of fused stalactites and stalagmites, each phosphorescent like the whole. The pool by which I had entered twisted and eddied, splashed into a broad waterfall which spread into a thin sheet over bright stones, and bubbled and foamed as it landed, creating a symphony of its own and causing luminous colors to flicker, deepening and brightening to the rhythm of its making. The exquisitely lighted walls were glassy smooth from being caressed by the musical flowing of waters which had formed them; and I knew this cavern symbolized the hall of music which was a part both of God and of the soul of every person.

As columns of mists formed, entirely different from the others and yet multicolored like them, and beauty, pain, and music intertwined, the rhythm of the music became outbursts of beauty, and the writhing of the pain became the rhythm of the music. Although I was literally inundated with multiple emotions, the deep reverence and all-encompassing love seemed to be the forces which caused the intertwining of the mists and the formation of another glistening pillar. This one took its place to the far left beside the pillar of true worth whose gems still sparkled like millions of tiny colored lights. Thereafter the placement of the glowing pillars alternated, one going to the right of the sky, the next to the left.

As if the halls of music and art were grouped with a third, I eddied directly into the cavern of creativity. Here stones containing bright oxides of minerals, miraculously translucent and lit from within, formed on various levels a vast network of rooms opening into one another, all different in shape, color, and cave structure. The luminous walls and icicle-like formations hanging from the ceiling gave one chamber a glow of warm yellow, another of mysterious blue, a third of reds ranging from delicate pink to rich maroon, and on through every shade of the color wheel, each room representing different creative arts and talents. When I realized I was looking at yet another God part of every person's soul, strong emotions again flooded through me. In awe and rapture I watched as another group of three exquisite columns of glistening mists formed a pillar of God, crying aloud and turning quickly to

Dr. Davidson while all four magnificent pillars still glowed in the sky.

During the last hour or more of the experience and for the remainder of the day, thoughts came with characteristic LSD rapidity; yet it seemed that except for my soul I had completely ceased to exist. In fact, nothing existed now but my soul and the deep religious feelings which poured forth in floods and torrents. Even the visions, as beautiful as they were, no longer appeared significant; they were merely the stimuli for spiritual emotions. Feelings and visions alike become cold and dead in the writing, a faint and shadowy account giving a prosaic one-hundred-thousandth of the experience itself.

These overpowering emotions quickly drove convictions deep into my soul. I was dead, and yet I was never more joyously alive; thus I knew that after death the soul is more alive than we can ever be while living. The overpowering presence of God which forced me to love all humanity cemented another conviction into place: since God is love, it is impossible to feel God within one's self without also loving all people. Though formerly I had accepted the belief that talent was a gift for only certain fortunate persons, a third conviction had come with the viewing of the caverns of art, music, and creativity: that every person possesses a tremendous fund of God-given talents.

I lay thinking that when talents remained unrecognized and unused, it was because of emotional blocks: children had been made to feel unworthy, inferior, and incapable of great accomplishments, and these strong emotions had remained throughout life. I recalled how often persons who expressed themselves in any type of creative art revealed such feeling by their fear of criticism and their longing for praise. It seemed to me that wasted potential was the greatest tragedy of life. As if intellectually reinforcing this LSD reverie, I remembered how fascinating it had been to watch talents come out of hiding when persons received good psychotherapy. Two friends with little training had won valued art prizes, others had learned to play musical instruments in relatively short periods, and still others had excelled on the stage and in myriad fields in which they had considered that they had no talent.

As my mind wandered on, it seemed to me that in one respect all creativity was equally valuable because it expressed the feelings of its creator. Who could say that one person's soul was more important than another's? Each person must express himself in whatever manner his interests and belief in self would allow him to, whether it be baking a cake, making a dress, doing needlepoint, or working with words, clay, paint, marble, or notes. I thought of a tablecloth worthy of a cathedral altar which a Mexican woman had crocheted for me. Although I knew her only by a sweet letter written in broken English, she had revealed her soul by her creativity and had given me a tremendous amount of her love.

Instantly there appeared before me, sparkling in the sun, a striking horn of plenty made of polished gold, so large it filled half the sky. From it spilled colossal apples, plums, peaches, bunches of grapes, and other fruits, each amazingly magnificent. Then from the horn came rolling billows of golden clouds tumbling to earth and covering the fruit. I knew that this sparkling golden mist symbolized God's love and that each person's horn of plenty was overflowing with love if he could but feel it. "God is love," was no mere Biblical quotation but an overwhelmingly intense burning into every nerve of my body. The wonder of it caused me both to soar with joy and to sob with pain.

Soon I was again a drop of water. Successively I trickled

into many caverns of varying shapes and sizes, each indescribably spectacular and each symbolic of another part of the soul. One huge cave held a mirror-smooth lake with a blue-black surface of satin richness, and in its depths were reflected in vivid detail the stalactite-covered dome. The whole was lit with an aurora borealis of flickering sapphire and lapis lazuli. This was the chamber of the unconscious where lay recorded all our past experiences and feelings, race history, universal wisdom, such power and strength as to assure us peace throughout all ages, and the depths and mysteries of life itself. An overpowering feeling of peace swept through me until I was saturated with serenity. As great blue columns formed and intertwined, the mists seemed to carry peace in their jewels, and the music, to carry peace in its whispers. I wept in thanksgiving as a pillar of luminous blue mists took its place with the others.

The thought occurred to me that, since every minute of our lives was ruled by our feelings, it was tragic we had so little contact with this part of ourselves where forgotten feelings lay hidden. Why did it have to be so difficult to read the ticker tape by which our actions revealed our unconscious minds? The expression, "Actions speak louder than words," showed we understood these actions to be unconsciously motivated, but the expression had become so trite that its tremendously important meaning was ignored.

There was no more time now for thinking. On I trickled into a delicate fairyland of slender stalagmites and stalactites beyond which I could see one lacy icicle-like formation after another. They appeared to be made of highly polished marble and were of various shades of pale pink, like an apple or almond orchard in party dress. The entire chamber was lit as if by sunshine which I knew to be the light of God. This cave symbolized tenderness and sweetness, both God elements in the soul of every human being. When the monumental pillar had formed of mists so soft in daintiness as to be delight in its purest form, there flashed before me a vivid picture of an incident of the previous Sunday.

At the close of church services, young parents had brought their infant for baptism. With them stood a couple so elderly that I had guessed them to be the baby's great-grandparents. Again I watched the minister as he handed what appeared to be a bundle of white fluff back to its mother and then baptized the aged man and his wife. With great gentleness he placed his hand on their white heads, spoke Christ's words with much tenderness, and kissed them both on their foreheads. This wonderful expression of sweetness and tenderness was so moving that tears ran down the cheeks of the elderly couple and those of the congregation as well. It seemed to me that these emotions had been all too rare in our lives; and that since we unconsciously feared direct and close relationships, our great hunger for human sweetness, tenderness, softness, and warmth made us seek these qualities in our clothing, blankets, rugs, and foods in the same way that our great longing for love made persons tragically grab at the vicarious straws of counterfeit in movies, TV shows, magazines, and novels.

Visions then appeared of a vast crowd of people, each holding a tiny earthenware urn ranging from 1 to 2 inches in diameter. The quantity an urn could hold symbolized the amount of love each person felt had been allotted to him. As they observed each other's urns, some were asking, "Why does he get more than I?" Instantly the sky was almost hidden by a tremendous golden urn with beautifully shaped handles on either side. Slowly the urn tipped, and from a pouring spout came God's love in the form of glistening golden clouds which floated to earth and inundated the multitude, showing there was more than enough of His love for everyone.

Gradually I became myself again. I sat up and stretched, noticing that bright bands of afternoon sunshine were coming through the venetian blinds. Waves of headache and nausea quickly swept over me. Even sitting up was an effort, and I soon lay down again and described the more recent visions to Dr. Davidson. Then for awhile I listened contentedly to the Gregorian Chants coming from the recorder.

My thoughts turned to the future of evolution, a subject which had fascinated me since the first LSD experience. I believed the time would eventually come when, without the use of drugs, each person would be in continuous contact with the beauty, the great capacity for love, the musical and artistic talents, the spiritual richness, and all the other wealth which now lay untapped deep inside himself. At this point the drug led me back underground.

In quick succession I, as a drop of water, eddied into several caverns symbolizing the same oneness of opposites which had revealed itself during the first and third experiences. One cave was formed of luminous stones which gave off red and maroon light symbolic of the positive aspects of hatred: that of giving depth to love and of making worth-while work possible. After a fantastically beautiful pillar of mist-borne rubies took its place, the golden urn reappeared. This time it poured forth red mists symbolic of hatreds which result from the frustrations of everyone's childhood and, though usually forgotten, are stored in the unconscious mind for a lifetime. Simultaneously there appeared, moving from left to right, groups of children playing with finger paints, clay, balls, toy hammers, and punching bags upon which the red mists first flowed, then evaporated. Instead of the urn emptying destructively on psychosomatic illnesses and crimes, the visions symbolized hatreds being harmlessly dissipated through hitting, kicking, and fantasy murders. Immediately the empty urn was refilled with the golden mists of love, showing that God's love fills the soul as soon as destructive hostilities can be gotten rid of.

The next two caverns, the first of lovely mellow grays and the second of radiant but soft yellows, symbolized the oneness of joy and sorrow and of happiness and unhappiness. Mists, glistening as if made of gems, formed columns and pillars and also poured forth from the great golden urn. After sorrow was emptied, the urn immediately filled with joy, and lovely iridescent gray mists representing this emotion streamed forth over the world. In the same manner the urn overflowed with soft yellow clouds as soon as unhappiness had poured out. It was strikingly clear that, until we are willing to experience the depths of our emotions, we can never know their heights. Many other caverns appeared showing the oneness of opposites, the urn repeatedly emptying itself of negative qualities, refilling, and then emptying the positive in full measure. It occurred to me that such expressions as "from the sublime to the ridiculous" and "I laughed till I cried" show that we do recognize the relation between opposites even though we customarily think of them as being different entities.

Dr. Davidson got up to put on more records, and I asked him to bring me a cup of beef broth. I sat up to drink it, wiping my eyes and nose between sips. The feelings of deep spirituality and tranquil reverence still hung over me like a pall. Christ's words, "In my Father's house are many mansions," kept coming into my mind, and I repeated them over and over. Despite the fact that I was well aware the sentence could be given many interpretations, to me at that moment the many mansions referred to the parts of the soul it was being my privilege to view.

Soon I seeped into a hall of faith which appeared to be formed entirely of white stone, somewhat chalky in appearance but flooded with light. Icicle-like formations of many different lengths, thicknesses, and shapes glistened with such millions of diamonds as to be unimaginable in splendor. The placement of these sparkling stalactites and stalagmites suggested semipartitions dividing the hall into hundreds of rooms symbolizing the many types of faith in the world; yet each compartment was brilliant with the light of God. As exquisite diamond-studded mists of silver white intertwined with such beauty as to cause tears to rain down my cheeks, God seemed comfortingly near. And I was convinced that faith too was a part of every person's soul regardless of how emphatically some individuals might deny it.

While the pillar of radiant silver mists took its place beside the others, it came to me that faith alone was not enough. Nor was a belief in God enough or the holding to a high moral code or to any form of worship or ritual. There must be a continuous spiritual growth, a constant searching deep within ourselves to free our intrinsic worth and our divine attributes, and a constant willingness to let our spiritual feelings live and grow. There came a renewed and even more unmovable conviction that deep religious experiences can be found only within ourselves. I could see now that the urge for growth, that upward but reversed God gravity I had felt so strongly during my first LSD session, applied to the development of the soul as much as to all other forms of evolvement.

Soon I found myself in the midst of a cavern where thousands of dainty translucent stalactites hung from the irregular ceiling. Even more stalagmites grew from the rough floor, each translucent and radiant, the whole flooded with delicate green lights which danced continuously. I realized that the fresh green color of spring and the ceaseless moving of the lights both symbolized the constant changes of spiritual growth. As green mists of infinite fragility rose glittering to the dome of heaven and coiled into another weightless pillar, I was convinced that if we were to know peace within ourselves, the need for spiritual development must be recognized, appreciated, and stressed far more than it now is in our culture.

Dr. Davidson left the room for a moment, and through the open door I could see that the afternoon was almost gone. An unrest seized me, and I was grateful when he returned, quickly throwing my hand over my head and taking his again. The emotions within me were too powerful to be endured alone.

When I had completely stopped crying, Dr. Davidson asked, "Would you like to bring me up to date?"

After summarizing the events since my last report, I commented, "Not only are the feelings utterly impossible to put into words, but who can describe a cave, let alone a dozen of them? I mean in such a way that a person who's never been in one can visualize it? I've been in only two caves in my life. One in North Dakota where everything was ugly and covered with thick dust and bats flew around your head. And the Oregon Caves. They were interesting but not in the slightest like the visions. Every cavern is different; yet all are aglitter, sparkling, saturated with light and color."

Dr. Davidson agreed that the task was a difficult one. Then we were silent. I kept wondering how one could accomplish spiritual growth, becoming more puzzled by the minute.

Again the curtain lifted, and I found myself in a cave filled with golden haze, so large as to be of breath-taking magnitude and grandeur. This was the hall of love, that part of the soul which is part of God Himself. Although irregular throughout, in size and shape it was somewhat like a huge opera house if viewed from the highest balcony. Semiscalloped tiers, slightly suggestive of lower balconies, showed below me. Walls and ceiling, stalactites and stalagmites alike sparkled with millions of tiny golden lights which winked on and off, as if the world's fireflies were congregated here. Far below, the lights became even smaller, and at the bottom there was only a soft, warm darkness, showing that none of us could ever know all of God's mysteries and measureless depths. The twinkling lights, I realized, showed that we allowed only a speck of God's love to shine through us at one time, quickly withdrawing it or turning it off at the least displeasure. Then as if every light had come on at once, the entire cavern was ablaze with splendor, this time revealing the brightness and true beauty of God which would shine if we allowed the love within us to glow to full capacity at all times. Even before the gleaming golden mists had intertwined beauty, pain, and music, and before the color had mellowed into a mist-made pillar of exquisite soft gold, the total impact was almost beyond enduring. My body shook with sobs, and while I held one of Dr. Davidson's hands in both of mine, he placed the other firmly against my head, sharing with me his sustaining strength.

As a drop of water I quickly found my way into two more caverns, both unutterable in loveliness. The first symbolized that part of our souls which recognized God as King. So rich was it in royal purples that I knew it was made entirely of amethysts. They were of many sizes and shapes, each brilliantly lit from within. The stalactites and stalagmites were so numerous that one appeared to represent each person who lives. It came to me that, since time began, every individual had somehow recognized God as King, regardless of how unaware he may have been of such cognizance or of what form of worship he employed. The conviction grew that God had existed long before primitive man had come and would exist after man had disappeared from the earth. As whirling mists of amethyst hues intertwined into a pillar of glistening purple, it seemed to me to be even more beautiful than any of the others.

The final cavern symbolized the eternal divinity of every person's soul and appeared to be made entirely of alabaster. Many stalagmites and stalactites had fused to form great irregular columns, and all were so translucent that soft lovely light passed through them. As I gazed at the marvels before me, I felt that somehow every person must be made to recognize the divine within himself and that such a recognition would influence his every action throughout life. It seemed to me that our lives were hopelessly confused and cluttered with mundane things of no real importance; and that the matter of greatest importance, the presence of a God part in each of us, lay within our reach at all times. If this potentiality were recognized and used, it would release for us unlimited strength, unlimited talents, unlimited harmony and peace, unlimited love, unlimited beauty, and the thousands of other qualities which we continuously search for. Then we would know that the kingdom of heaven was truly within us where Christ had so often told us it could be found.

Such thoughts were blotted out while glittering mists of alabaster jewels formed a pillar of the divinity in man. As I sobbed, I felt devotion to God far greater than I had ever experienced before and seemingly greater than any person had the capacity to hold. This pillar filled the one remaining gap between the others, each of which was evenly spaced across the entire sky. There now stood fourteen gigantic pillars of luminous mists, all harmonious in shade and brilliance: those of multicolored gems and rainbow hues, and one each of royal purple, pale yellow, delicate green, apple-blossom pink, red with miniature rubies, jeweled gray, diamond-studded silver, delicate gold, and lastly the glistening white of God's purity. Even after the majestic pillars faded from view, I could still see colored shadows across the night sky.

When the curtain dropped, I found myself wishing that every living person might be given LSD and see beauty equal to that which I had witnessed, have the same feelings, and know the blessed nearness of God. Even more, I wished that these feelings might stay uppermost in all of us at all times. Then wars could never again be fought, crimes would cease, and fears and distrusts would disappear from the earth.

CHAPTER 12

My Cup Runneth Over

THE FIFTH and last LSD experience had already been divided into two distinct parts: the aboveground adventures of a drop of water, and the caverns of the soul. These aspects of the soul were now set aside for a time, although I was to see them again later.

During the remainder of the day, all my emotions became progressively more overpowering. I had not realized before to what an extent such feelings as rapture, delight, ecstasy, and euphoria, or awe, devotion, reverence, and holiness or any other positive emotion could reach before its intensity changed it to agony, despair, torment, and excruciating pain. Even commonplace thoughts and simple visions seemed to be the stimuli for violent emotions. Deeply religious feelings, however, stayed continuously uppermost, rising with no apparent stimuli.

When pain became severe, Dr. Davidson held my hand, pressing it tightly and sharing his strength with me. Many times he placed his other hand on my head, caressingly or firmly, as my needs demanded. It seemed to me that his hands deadened pain like an anesthetic and that the love of all humanity and the peace of God flowed through them.

As if to give myself strength for the experience yet to come, I lay resting quietly and then asked Dr. Davidson to bring me a cup of broth. I had been repeatedly surprised to find that I had definite ideas as to what the soul was; now as I sipped the steaming bouillon, my thoughts turned to what the soul was not. It seemed to me that personality would be discarded at death in somewhat the same way an Easter hat we thought so lovely a year ago loses favor; the part of the mind given to trivial things surely had no immortality; and the ego, which continuously pushed us about trying to satisfy its selfish wants, would be dissolved, and good riddance. At this point I could feel the drug taking over, and with it came another conviction: not until we could set aside the ego, either by satisfying its merciless demands or by recognizing its relative unimportance, could we achieve spiritual growth here on earth.

Before me came an African medicine man, old, wrinkled, superstitious, yet wise in many ways. And then I was he. A moment later I both saw and became an Eskimo woman, kind, full of yearning, and deeply concerned for my children and husband; an Indian maharajah sitting in an ornate room, feeling both the emptiness of wealth and a hunger for something I could not identify; and an Australian aborigine, asking little of life, yet loving it as much as anyone on earth. In this manner a vast montage of persons passed before me, and I was each in turn, young and old, primitive and highly cultured, wealthy and without possessions.

For every one of these persons I had great compassion, a tremendous understanding, and an almost infinite love. As some, I knew a spiritual poverty, as others, a spiritual development beyond my comprehension, but as all, a longing for further spiritual growth. This feeling made me realize as never before that the need for spirituality was a universal need of every individual who lives. Yet each had been the receiver of God's love to such an extent that another conviction came: God values all life with absolute equality. It came to me that God was singularly unimpressed by the color of skin, the size of a bank account, the number of college degrees, the placement in beauty contests, the status with the Joneses, and a million similar things by which we strive to give ourselves a sense of importance. With these feelings there came for me a new sense of values, a stopping to ask myself again and again, "What is it that's truly important?"

In spite of the fact that I had seemed to become one with each individual who lives, I still had the feeling of floating weightless and bodiless. Then I realized I was the soul of each living person. Although my thoughts, reactions, and words continued to be my own, during the remainder of the experience it seemed to me that, as the soul of any bit of humanity, I was without ego, without selfishness, and without concern for any trivial thing. At the same time I was the receiver of God's love to such an overwhelming degree that to love all humanity was a compulsory rule impossible to violate, a feeling so wonderful as to be painful to endure.

These hundreds of visions and feelings seemed to come in a flash, and now when I felt God's love so overpoweringly, I stretched my arms upward and outward, wanting to hug to myself all who live. Then gratitude filled me; dropping my hands quickly, I placed my palms together over my chest, crying out between choking sobs, "Thank you, God! Thank you! Thank you!"

From my hands there grew to heaven a glorious Eiffel Tower of golden mists. Beneath it, passing from left to right, I saw persons praying: children in nightdress at bedside, light gleaming on tiny bowed heads, flaxen, brown, and black; blessings asked around family tables; the Pilgrims expressing sincere gratitude for the bounty of their first Thanksgiving; and the Mormons asking God's help in making a desert, unwanted by others, bloom with His goodness. There were persons of every nationality and faith praying in churches, cathedrals, synagogues, temples, and mosques. Of those who knelt in pews and at altars during the week, there were far more Catholics than Protestants. I watched primitive man worship the sun, lightning, fire, and rain and early nomads worship the spirits of forests, clouds, and rivers. Before me came the Greeks and Romans worshiping Chaos, Ceres, Gaea, Uranus, Neptune, Apollo, Venus, Vesta, Diana, and Aurora. These gods and goddesses of creation, growth, earth, heaven, sea, sun, love, fire, moon, and dawn, respectively, were every one a part of the God whom we ourselves worship. It seemed to me that regardless of what symbols were used, all men through all ages had worshiped exactly the same God; and that these early men were perhaps nearer the meaning of God and less vague about Him than we ourselves are at times.

Then came a vision magnificent both to see and to contemplate. Every person who lives in the world today was shown with hands joined in the Friends' fashion of asking a blessing. Americans held the hands of Russians; Russians the hands of the people of Laos; the Laotians, the hands of native Africans; the Africans, the hands of the Dutch and Belgians; and on through every race and every nation. Enemies no longer existed. Together all the world's population formed a great wreath which spiraled again and again around our entire globe, the spiral stretching from north to south pole. Together they thanked God for peace among us all, a realizable purpose of His creation. As I watched, love which I had felt overpoweringly throughout the day multiplied until I seemed to be experiencing the sum total of love in the soul of every person who lives. God's love was a very real thing, a thousand times more real than the davenport upon which I lay. Like sap running from roots to trunk to branches to leaves, it filled every molecule in my body to bursting, becoming excruciating in its magnitude.

For a long time I lay sobbing, shaken to the core by the violent feelings, and thinking for the hundredth time that it was unbelievable that so much love had lain hidden within myself or could exist in any human being. Then I asked Dr. Davidson to bring me coffee and sat quivering as I drank it.

My glance fell on a copy of *The Prophet* by Kahlil Gibran which lay on the table beside me. I had brought it that morning because several persons had said that when under the drug they had understood parts of Shakespeare, the Bible, and Omar Khayyam which had been meaningless to them before. Now it seemed impossible to hold the book, much less to read it. More in an attempt to escape soul-shaking emotions than to gain new insights, I asked Dr. Davidson if he would read it to me.

For a few moments he thumbed through the book, then in a pleasant voice full of expression, he read: "Your children are not your children. They are the sons and daughters of life's longing for itself."

Instead of subduing my feelings, my emotions thrashed violently in first one direction and then another, like a week's wash being mercilessly whipped by a terrific gale. I had been so carried away by my feelings that I had not even thought of my children all day. Now the total fullness of God's love seemed to pour out on them, and I watched a quick rerun of the caverns of the soul with them standing in the center of each. The recognition of the divinity of their souls filled me with overwhelming awe and reverence toward them. Then I sobbed with remorse; that very morning I had been angry with my son for not feeding his dog, and with my young daughter for spilling unfrozen orange-juice popsicles each containing nearly a bottleful of a different food coloring over the sides and bottom of the freezer. Even the magic of LSD could not blot out the memory of the vile-colored Persian rug of ice. Now these things were infinitely trivial. I prayed that I might fulfill the children's emotional needs by giving them love, tenderness, softness, and warmth; that I might aid and stimulate their spiritual growth and protect them only when they required it, thus allowing freedom for them to develop as God intended they should.

Dr. Davidson was reading: "You are the bows from which your children as living arrows are sent forth."

It seemed to me that God was also the bow, and we, regardless of age, were the children, the living arrows sent forth; that we must always remain children, thus to continue growth throughout our entire lives. Surely Christ's words, "Except ye be converted, and become as little children, ye shall not enter into the kingdom of heaven," referred to the necessity for continuous spiritual growth which alone could lead to the joy of fulfillment He had spoken of as heaven.

When I listened again, Dr. Davidson was reading, "What have you in these houses? Have you peace, the quiet urge that reveals your power?"

Immediately I was saturated with peace, a feeling so wonderful that it took the path from joy to pain. Yet I could not understand how peace could be an urge which revealed power and asked Dr. Davidson to explain it.

"Only strength can give the security which brings peace," he replied.

Instantly I thought of the God strength which had both filled and sustained me during the trip over Niagara Falls. Although the feeling of peace remained all pervading, I simultaneously experienced a soul-shaking power. The power was so great that it seemed atomic bombs could not touch it, the peace so secure that it would reign throughout all eternity.

"Wars will come and go," I thought. "They are as much a tragic part of evolution as was the fighting in the marshes. Yet they are but a flicker of an eyelash of eternity. Eventually we shall evolve to the stage where peace will exist forever and ever."

Suddenly a great beam of light focused on me, and against a background of darkness I became an exploding atomic bomb which tore my body asunder yet showed me unutterable beauty. With spherical, all-directional vision, I watched millions of sparks fly from me, each exploding into two; each of these sped on, splitting in geometric ratio until the entire universe seemed filled with glorious fire of infinitely delicate design and loveliness. Viewed at 360 degrees in every direction, the display was breath-taking in both speed and magnitude. While I watched a universe aglitter with fountains of falling sparks, I knew I had been given some small insight of the strength upon which God's peace was built. There followed blessed darkness, as soothing as a cool night after a sun-scorched day.

When I could listen once more, Dr. Davidson was reading about prayer. It occurred to me that our every act was in reality a prayer. Our work was a prayer for greater bounty. The desire to excel was often a prayer for approval. In one way or another, prayers for love were hidden in most of our actions. Since stored anger must be released before the feelings of love can live, even a curse seemed to me to be a prayer for love.

Then I heard the words, "And an old priest said, 'Speak to us of religion.' And he said, 'Have I spoken this day of aught else?' "

It seemed to me that our religion was our every deed,

every breath, and every thought; that cheating on income tax was as much our religion as the check we sent to the church; and that prejudices toward Negro, Jew, or Catholic reflected our religion far more than did our Sunday worship. To think of religion as confined to church attendance was a mockery and a hypocrisy. Again the conviction came that religion was a deep inner need of every person who ever lived, a soul crying for spiritual growth and fulfillment.

So strong were my feelings that I wanted to become a Billy Graham, to attract great crowds, and to tell them religion was a living, vital core inside every person. Never was I more sincere, nor was I the first who under LSD had wanted to be a deliverer. I had no time now to listen to reading. But for a second I thought sympathetically of the many well-meaning persons who had wished to share some fulfillment of theirs with me by sending me religious pamphlets, recalling that after a single mail had brought literature on Mormonism, Zen Buddhism, Jehovah's Witnesses, and the Oxford Group, my secretary had remarked, "If you want to please your public, you'll have to join every church and sect."

Now in a voice similar to that used by ministers at the height of revivals I had attended as a child, I started to preach a sermon to a vast audience which suddenly appeared before me. Simultaneously it came to me that, since a part of God was in each of us, we saw the God within ourselves every time we looked in the mirror.

"What kind of God is it you see in your mirror?" I cried with tremendous emphasis. "Has He granite eyes and hard lines about His mouth? Or do your eyes show His kindness, sweetness, compassion, and love? Does your face show His softness, warmth, and charity? Can you see God's greatness in your smile, or is it a mockery, a forced imitation of emotions you cannot feel?" Then my voice rose even higher.

"Study God's face in your mirror! See what your God is like. Then work till your dying day to let more of His face shine through!"

It did not occur to me at the time that the audience was made up of different aspects of myself. Instead I thought of the amount of God which showed in the faces of my friends. Although I had been brought up a Protestant and had little contact with other churches, it seemed to me that God shone in the faces of Catholics far more than in Protestant faces. Similarly persons in Catholic nations, such as Austria, Spain, Italy, and Mexico, let more of God shine through than do the people of Protestant countries.

Again I started shouting, sincere to the tips of my toenails and feeling that no minister had ever experienced greater devotion to God. "Would that we could all live our faith as joyously as do devout Catholics! Since Christ no longer walks the earth, it is the responsibility of every person who professes faith to show by deeds and actions, by kindnesses, warmth, and love, that God indeed still lives. Then persons who know or care little for Him can see and feel and want Him."

For a moment the cavern symbolic of the soul's urge for spiritual growth reappeared before me, quickly followed by the luminous silver-white chambers of faith.

"Why haven't we enough faith in our King to pattern our lives after Christ's?" I demanded, sobbing with the violence of my emotions. "I can tell you one reason: college philosophy courses require you to read the works of God-denying and pessimistic philosophers in which every belief one held as a child is questioned. Such courses are often taught by equally God-denying and pessimistic professors. After the props are cruelly knocked from under the student, he is given no substitute but is left with a heartful of yearnings. It seems to me such courses ruthlessly destroy faith, and in this respect I believe colleges often do more harm than good.

"This morning I saw a Mexican woman praying in a tiny church. She probably had never received one day of education. Yet I suspect she is nearer her God than are most college graduates today."

When I stopped to reach for a facial tissue, Dr. Davidson commented that he was sorry he had not set up a tape recorder.

Ignoring his remark, I quickly focused my anger on the exaltation of science with its premise that everything had to be proved.

"Our so-called scientific attitude destroys faith and throttles spiritual development," I told my audience with grave emphasis. Then I raised my voice, shouting, "Things of real worth can never be proved: God, love, compassion, mercy, kindness, charity, and dozens of other wonderful values. Faith is the acceptance of these values, supposedly without proof, but the proof lies in the deep wisdom within you. The worship of science has caused us to underestimate things of lasting worth and to lose confidence in our own innate wisdom."

When not under LSD, I normally respect scientists, but now a vision came before me showing them as ants scurrying rapidly around a tiny anthill. I turned back to my audience, my voice calmer now as I resumed preaching.

"As eons pass, it will perhaps be noted that Einstein stated the theory of relativity in 1905 and that the hydrogen bomb was first tested in 1956 in much the same way that Columbus's discovery of 1492 is now spoken of." I stopped to pound my fist against the table as I spoke the next sentence. "But God, faith, love, hope, and charity will remain long after science and philosophy have been forgotten. These are the values of lasting worth to hold always close to your heart."

Once more I became an exploding bomb while before my eyes the gods of science and the God-denying philosophies were destroyed. Again I watched with the miracle of all-directional vision as the magnificence of God's strength revealed itself. There came over me such a trust as must fill a small, unhurt child, a joyous and tranquil thing, and an optimism sank into my very being, never again to be daunted.

The wave passed, but the tremendous love I now felt for God and for all humanity stayed with me. It seemed to me it was this feeling of love which had prompted the outpouring of my words.

Then, as during and after every experience, my mind turned in awe and amazement to wondering where such insights and overpowering emotions could come from. I thought of how persons who had not taken the drug argued that such material must originate entirely in the subject's own background, understanding, knowledge, yearnings, and conflicts, pointing out that anyone ignorant of evolution could not have lived it as I had. Individuals who had been richly rewarded by LSD invariably argued with equal vigor that material unrelated to one's life experience did at times present itself. Certainly the many convictions, feelings, and insights I had had this day had not come from my past; and every experience had caused me to run to the encyclopedia to check the accuracy of material. For example, I had been repeatedly surprised at how often Buddha and Mohammed had come up, although I had known almost nothing of either. I had not even been aware that Brahma was the name for God in the Hindu religion but thought it a type of cattle. Unrecognized sources of wisdom did seem to be set free by the drug.

The sensation of bodiless and weightless floating once more took over, and I was again the soul of any living person. For the next two hours or more I repeated many Biblical quotations, gaining far deeper understanding of God and of Christ's words than I had ever had before. Again and again I wondered why I had not comprehended meanings which now seemed so obvious. Since in my opinion each person must find the type of worship which best meets his individual needs and since Biblical meanings easily lend themselves to argument, I am purposely omitting these interpretations.

During this period hundreds of visions passed before my eyes, and dozens of Old Testament characters again lived and breathed. Later I repeated the Lord's Prayer and the Twenty-Third Psalm over and over. With each repetition, the words became more meaningful, more wrought with comfort, forgiveness, and God's love. Yet meanings were merely incidental compared to the monumental emotions which reached their peak during this period, becoming unimaginably deep and soul shaking. Much of the time I cried aloud, often writhing with pain which nevertheless contained a great component of joy, but gaining tremendous comfort from the pressure of Dr. Davidson's hands.

When reality came again, I noticed that darkness had fallen. Dr. Davidson mentioned that he would have to leave in half an hour to see a patient, adding, "What an experience! This is a day you'll never forget."

As it turned out, I was alone only a few moments before Frank came for me. I assured him again and again that he had never been loved as I loved him then. After we reached home, I saw no more visions; perhaps the violence of the emotions caused them to burn themselves out early. In the short time remaining, however, a single spectacular vision seemed a fitting climax to all five experiences.

When the drug claimed me for the last time, I saw Christ standing before me. He spoke the words recorded in the Gospel according to St. Matthew, "I am with you alway," and they rang with such monumental truth that I wondered how we could ever for a moment forget His promise. Then He spoke again, "Peace I leave with you, my peace I give unto you."

Even as every molecule in my body was filling with such a glorious and soothing peace that it amounted to euphoria, I knew He had given me a thousand times more than peace alone. He had given me and every other living person His forgiveness, His compassion, His tenderness, and His love.

Again there came before me the magnificent Eiffel Tower of love which reached to the dome of heaven, but this time its golden brilliance was so glorious that it blinded me for a moment. Or was it the love that I felt which blinded me?

While I rubbed my eyes, I realized I had been granted a wish I had expressed in a poem years earlier. I had called it *Blind Me with Love.* As the great golden tower shimmered before me, I quoted it to Dr. Davidson.

They say that love is blind. How strange!
To me, love's eyes are sparkling bright.

Love sees beauty in faces the world calls homely
And often tragedy in faces the world calls beautiful.

Love sees fear behind fits of temper
And understands that anger is but the outward expression of fears which lie quaking in the heart.

Love sees softness beneath rough exterior and brusque manner
And knows the greater the brusqueness and roughness, the greater the tenderness within.

Love sees pain behind the laughter of the brave

And realizes that merriment hides hurts from him whose sorrow well is already overflowing.

Love sees sadness in the alcoholic's stupor
And pities the need to deaden unasked-for shame and guilt and failure.

Love sees joys through tears of sorrow
And recognizes that the greater the sadness, the greater the joy can be.

Love sees release in the death of the weary,
When to mother earth and her tender womb we each return.

Love sees the outstretched arms of hungry humanity,
Begging for the love which could fulfill its inner cravings.

Love sees the need to give abundantly of itself
For its own maintenance and sustenance.

Love sees in such abundant giving
Peace upon earth for all mankind.

To me, love's eyes are sparkling bright;
But if love be blind, O God,
Blind me this hour and for all the hours through time.
Blind me with eternal love.

As I spoke the last lines, they became a prayer that the love I had experienced throughout the day might stay with me for all the hours through time.

Then there came a quick rerun of the caverns of the soul, but this time already formed pillars took their places in the sky. At last the heavens were all but filled with luminous mists so rich in color as to be a marvel never to be forgotten. As I watched, all the mist-made pillars changed to a mellow, glistening gold. Simultaneously there appeared beneath them a broad foundation of burnished gold standing on a low mountain; above, a golden roof glistened in God's light. The total appearance was that of a sky-wide and sky-high acropolis, awesome in its magnitude. This I knew was the sacred temple of the soul, not of mine alone but of every human being who lives.

As if in rhythm to my shaking sobs, the words I had repeated earlier in the afternoon re-echoed in my mind, "My cup runneth over. Surely goodness and mercy shall follow me all the days of my life."

CHAPTER 13

Aftermaths and Rewards

PERSONS frequently ask, "What's the value of LSD?"

It is a natural enough question, but to me it seems an extremely difficult one to answer. Instead of replying directly, I find myself wanting to ask, "What's the value of watching a glorious sunset? Of listening to magnificent music? Of visiting the great art galleries? Of world travel? Of soaring on a paean of joy? Of feeling a unity with all life? Of knowing the pain of too much loving? Of being given insight into the greatness of the soul of man? Of worship and reverence and feeling the nearness and strength of God? And of losing one's self in devotion to Him?" Anyone who can answer these questions and dozens of similar ones will have my reply as to the value of LSD.

For a few short but forever unforgettable hours LSD gives one the love of God, the forgiveness of Christ, the humility of St. Francis, the intellect of Einstein, and the compassion of Allah, the All Compassionate. Have these experiences value? I believe they have.

It seemed to me that Helen, who took the drug with me the first time, wrote of value in her report: "The doctor gave me an injection of lysergic acid, but he also gave me heaven and earth and eternity. In that infinitesimal drop of chemical lay a magic key to paradise, a paradise of beauty and depth of knowing and understanding which had lain dormant within me. I felt a wonderful new optimism and a sense of peace and harmony and letting be. I knew that everything fits, everything is in its place, and everything is part of a harmonious whole; and that the human soul has measureless depths. The infinite sadness and indescribable beauty of all humanity which I was feeling and seeing reached so high that they joined and were part of God, leaving me worshipful and reverent. My tears were born in the very depths of my soul to express this infinite sadness and exquisite beauty; yet there was no torment in my crying. Instead I felt that I had been given a trust which I must never lose and yet must share with everyone."

Are these emotions valuable? I believe they are.

During a government investigation of the use of peyote by the Native American Church, an Indian made the statement, "You white men go to your church house and talk about God. We eat peyote and talk with God."

To me his remark also summarizes the value of LSD. Persons who have had religious experiences under the drug no longer merely talk about God. For them He is forever afterward a vital, throbbing force which cannot help but influence their lives. Just as a glorious sunset will always be remembered even though it cannot be recalled in all its breath-taking grandeur, the total impact of an LSD experience can never be forgotten regardless of how much the visions may dim. An acquaintance given the drug years ago recently remarked, "You're never the same once you've had LSD. It makes life take on richer meanings."

Someone once asked Benjamin Franklin what electricity

was good for. He replied, "What's the value of a newborn baby?"

LSD is indeed a newborn baby, and its real worth can probably not be foreseen as yet any more than the many uses of electricity could have been known in 1790.

As Dr. Davidson pointed out in the Introduction, the evaluation of a drug which affects the mind is extremely difficult for the hundreds of psychiatrists doing LSD research. Dr. Janiger hoped to evaluate it by information gained from a follow-up of page after page of questions sent to approximately 800 subjects who had taken the drug under his guidance. As a probing scientist, he wanted to know such things as reactions following the experiences, willingness to take the drug again, and the respect in which it appeared to be the most helpful. He asked what changes were noticed, if any, in personality traits, creativity, sexual expression, and interpersonal relationships; in understanding or interests in a variety of subjects such as art, music, history, and anthropology; and in one's sense of values pertaining to money, possessions, and knowledge. And on and on through hundreds of questions.

When the drug is taken while one is undergoing psychotherapy, it is almost impossible to be specific as to which of the two has brought about various changes in attitudes, feelings, and personality. Nevertheless, my response to Dr. Janiger's questionnaire summarizes as nearly as I can my opinion of the values I received from being given LSD.

A year has now passed since I first ventured behind the curtain; yet I still consider the five days under the drug to be the most important ones of my life. In my case, no visions appeared except on the days LSD was given me, but during the week following each experience I often burst unexpectedly into growls and snarls, vigorous galloping movements, silkworm undulations, or cobra hisses. The day after I had lived through evolution, I was utterly exhausted. Some twelve hours of interplanetary travel caused my little-used galloping muscles to stay extremely painful for about two weeks, and my persistent eating of "mulberry leaves" resulted in my jaws becoming so sore that I had to live on baby food a few days. These discomforts were minor indeed compared to the compensations.

The second day after my initial experience found me feeling buoyant, tremendously released, and unusually happy, a reaction which lasted approximately a month, during which I wanted to think and talk of nothing except the wonders of LSD. I found myself watching people with a new fascination, admiring their courage and nobility, and feeling a wondrous compassion, understanding, and love for them. Regardless of how low on the evolutionary ladder any individual appeared to be, I could not forget that deep within was an admirable human being with an unlimited capacity for love. The second experience resulted in both a month-long, optimistic, glorious rapture which amounted to euphoria, and an amazing outburst of "universal energy"; I felt inexhaustible, continuously fresh, and rested despite little sleep. A markedly noticeable increase in the appreciation of beauty followed the silkworm experience. Not only did almost any lovely object take on still more graceful lines, often becoming luminous and sparkling with jewels, but I could see beauty in hundreds of commonplace things I had not thought of as being even attractive before. Such emotions as tolerance, understanding, love for humanity, unity with all life, and awareness of God's nearness came with the first experience and were strengthened by each of the others.

The positive emotions of each experience I relived again and again: the glorious ascension to heaven, the serenity of paradise, the joyous galloping from planet to planet, the carefree dance of the fairies, and particularly the peace which followed the last experience. Recently, as I watched a spectacular sunset, I was once again the queen of the silkworms unfurling fabulous skyfuls of glorious colors. In contrast, such feelings as the sufferings of the insane, the terror of the marshes and of the cobra's attack, or the excruciating death of the Christian martyr have never been repeated. Unfortunately I was not able to remember the original melodies which I considered so magnificent, although a musician would possibly have perfect recall.

Many of my reactions to the drug were surprising indeed. For example, within a week after my first sojourn into other worlds I noticed that I seemed to have two personalities: a pre-LSD personality in which my own feelings stayed dominant and to which I reverted under stress; and a post-LSD personality characterized by serenity, tolerance, optimism, and a forgetfulness of self. When the latter personality was uppermost, I could at times sense the feelings of others with an amazingly accurate intuition. The two personalities became more evident with each experience, but after a period of months they apparently became amalgamated and were no longer separately recognizable.

A persistent sensation completely new to me, glorious in its novelty and yet seeming to be unbearably conceited, followed the Pegasus experience. I felt that I was beautiful. If all the faces in the world were to be put into a grab bag and each of us was given another chance, I would be afraid to take it; yet no one has ever nominated me as a Miss America candidate. The emotion, however, persisted tenaciously for weeks until I finally realized that I was actually experiencing the awareness of the God beauty inside every human being. This seemingly egotistical and unimportant aftermath caused me to become even more aware that beauty does exist within every person, and I suspect it will influence my interpersonal relationships as long as I live.

During this same period, I sat alone one night watching the flame of an unusually beautiful candle. "That's God!" I suddenly exclaimed aloud with rapidly mounting excitement, the new conviction that God pervaded all things fresh within me. For several days I was like a two-year-old playing peek-aboo and saying "I see You!" at each new discovery. I saw Him alike in the faces of my children, husband, and friends and even strangers; in the ocean, trees, flowers, insect wings, clouds, and the water bubbling over rocks as it enters our pool. He was in the notes of music, the songs of birds, and the clang of cowbells and church bells. God, Who had always been so vague and remote before, was now real and near; and I knew He would never again be invisible to me. Thus I was given another rich and lasting reward.

Although I already considered my relationship with my husband and children a good one, considerable improvement was apparent following several experiences. After my stay in paradise where I thought of the children as jewels, I seemed to have the ability to love them more than I had realized was possible. At the same time I was more intuitive of their feelings and thus more compassionate and understanding of them. During this period I repeatedly saw their faces glow as if lit from within, an amazing phenomenon which friends and neighbors even noticed and commented upon. When I went to take LSD the second time, my nine-year-old daughter told my secretary, "My mommie has gone to take the drug which makes her terribly nice for a whole month."

The ecstasy of the Pegasus experience caused joy to pervade our home for weeks. Even a state of disorder reminded me that pleasant emotions were more important than neatness and that somehow my "universal energy" had to be used up. To the children's regret and mine, this easy-going attitude soon wore off. The lingering confusion of the silkworm experience and the depressing quality of the cobra's attack caused me to draw into my own thoughts and probably left the children feeling rejected for a while. Our family life reached near utopia for a short time, however, after the last experience in which it became impossible not to love all mankind, and every member of the family responded generously, returning warmth for warmth. Unfortunately, by the end of a month, love of this extreme intensity had taken on a will-o'-the-wisp quality, but LSD had opened wide the door through which love passes, and it was left ajar.

One of the greatest values of the drug to me was the feeling that it was literally impossible not to love every person who lives, an emotion which, I am convinced, is a real feeling of God within ourselves. Since intercourse is a form of expressing deep love provided the marriage partners are reasonably mature emotionally, the intensity of the love feelings caused sexual hungers and reactions to be markedly heightened. For a time intercourse took on such depth of meaning as to have a religious significance.

It is difficult for me to evaluate changes in human relationships outside the family group. Since the drug experiences, I feel that I am less critical and considerably more tolerant, sympathetic, forgiving, and understanding, but I have no idea whether other people are aware of these feelings in me. In the abstract, the feeling of loving all humanity is still strong, but in reality I find that it breaks down all too quickly if I have annoying contacts with persons whom I do not care to be with.

Dr. Janiger's question, "Have you noticed any difference in your interest in anthropology or history?" meets with my hearty, "Indeed I do." Formerly I found it extremely difficult to imagine the feelings of anyone whose living conditions or culture differed markedly from our own; examples would be anyone who lived several hundred years ago or a primitive alive today. Under LSD I was repeatedly all humanity, experiencing its hungers, yearnings, hatreds, terrors, and illnesses, its love, appreciation, reverence, tranquillity, and ecstasy. As a result I have a wonderful, crazy feeling, admittedly without basis of reality, that I have been in every person's shoes. This emotion has given a pulsating aliveness and a throbbing heartbeat to history and anthropology and has tremendously increased my interest in both. Partly as a result of these identifications, I am convinced that the emotions of all persons from prehistoric man to the modern sophisticate are essentially the same. Some people certainly suppress their feelings more than do others, some are more sensitive, and the lives of different individuals vary widely indeed, but the actual emotions themselves, I believe, remain identical and universal.

Changes in my sense of values after the drug experiences have also been marked and surprising. Money has become far less important, and even paying taxes no longer annoys me. As a friend says, "Hell, it's nothing but money." Possessions too have become less valuable. Except for necessities, I want to own little aside from beautiful things which, as manifestations of God, can keep us mindful of His presence. Formerly I placed the well-informed, educated person at the top of the heap, but my vote would now be quickly cast for the person with the greatest outgoing warmth. I feel that only an individual who is relatively mature both emotionally and spiritually has the ability to give genuine love uncontaminated by self-interest.

The effect of LSD on the creative urge was for me immediate and marked. Although I have had eight books published and two manuscripts were well under way, I had not wanted to write for four or five years. My first LSD report was scarcely finished when I found myself wanting to paint, practice the piano, start a new book, follow my hobby of working with plastics, and do a variety of other creative things. The drive was so strong as to be compulsive, resulting in much frustration because of limited time. Furthermore it increased with each subsequent experience and has not subsided throughout the intervening year. When this urge first made itself felt, I had not yet heard of Dr. Janiger's findings that composers given the drug discovered that they had greater insight into music, that art judges acclaimed paintings done after the drug experience to be superior to those executed before it, or that writers, artists, and musicians alike had found that it increased their creativity.

An easy question to answer was, "Would you be willing to take the drug again?"

If I might rub an Aladdin's lamp, I would make a wish that all persons who desired to take LSD could do so, and that I might be given it approximately twice each year, although not at regular intervals. In my opinion, its greatest value can be obtained by taking it at specific times, perhaps best shown by an incident my husband told me about after a recent trip into Mexico.

In a tiny village high in the mountain peaks where Mr. Wasson first investigated the magic mushroom, Frank was talking to an Indian girl. "Have you eaten the mushrooms?" he asked her.

"No," she replied.

"Do you know persons who have eaten them?"

"*Si, si*. Many of them."

"Are you afraid? Is that why you haven't eaten them?"

"No. *Por spiritu.*" She searched for English words. "They are for persons who are sick in the soul. My soul is not sick."

I should like to be given LSD at times when my soul is sick, when I find I am not able to express love as generously as I wish I might, when my creativity is at a low ebb, or when I am dragging my spiritual heels. The drug, used as an aid to psychotherapy, has already been valuable to many persons who were sick in the soul.

Another question easy to answer was, "In what way do you feel the drug has been most helpful to you?"

Although the experiences have been fulfilling in hundreds of ways, by far the most meaningful have been the religious insights and feelings of spirituality. The last experience was unutterably rewarding in this respect; the other four have taken on greater religious significance as time passes. For example, not long ago a friend laughingly referred to my galloping from planet to planet. To my surprise, I was instantly shocked and hurt. When one sees God as light and beauty penetrating the whole of the universe, feelings are far too intense and sacred to contain one iota of humor.

The experiences have caused me to become interested in many forms of worship and in churches of every denomination. Each time I passed a church for months, I not only longed to attend services but to become part of the congregation; hence the year has taken me into many churches of many faiths. The time I have had for reading has been given almost entirely to the study of various religions, and a dozen books on the subject are now stacked on my bedside table. My interest in the Bible has increased, particularly in learning meaningful quotations from it. These reactions are minor indeed, however, compared to the fulfilling and lasting feelings of reverence and spirituality, the awareness of the continuous presence of God, and the conviction that nothing can be difficult as long as we remember Christ's words, "I am with you alway." It seems to me that if a person is to know peace, he must find a faith by which he can live and gain rich fulfillment.

Dr. Marcus Bach[3] has expressed both the point of view I arrived at through the drug experiences and the tolerance I believe we should each hold for the religious views of another: "There is one God; He is known by many names. There is one faith; it is lived in many beliefs. There is one truth; it is seen through many minds. There is one worship; it is expressed in many forms."

I have heard it argued that one obtains from LSD whatever he is looking for, and that a person not interested in religion would have no mystical experiences. This point of view I disagree with heartily, thinking particularly of a report written by a man who stated that he had been an atheist before taking the drug but that he could never be again. Certainly this man was not looking for a religious experience. A rather large per cent of persons given LSD have religious experiences, and peyote and certain mushrooms whose effects are similar have been used in religious ceremonies for hundreds of years. It seems to me that in this day when spiritual hungers and longings are both widespread and acute, LSD has a great potential in the field of religious development alone.

As a result of this spiritual fulfillment, an amazingly deep new optimism has come to me. Formerly when I felt the hot breath of Communism on my neck, read the daily paper, thought of our national debts, or listened to discussions of world affairs or governmental corruption, I was thrown into a miserable depression, agreeing with Spengler that the West

[3] Bach, Marcus. *Faith and My Friends*. Indianapolis: Bobbs-Merrill Company, 1951.

was indeed declining. My reaction now is, considering the short time man has been on earth, that he has made fantastic progress in every field. Certainly much remains to be done, and undoubtedly tragic fighting as in the marshes will still occur. But to one who accepts the God pull of reversed gravity and maintains a geological time sense, the future seems gloriously bright.

The most lasting value of the drug experiences for me appears to be a number of convictions, most of them religious in nature, which are so strong that it makes not one iota of difference whether anyone agrees with them or not. I cannot shake them even though some are inconsistent with logical thinking. For example, time becomes real indeed each morning as the school bus nears our corner, although my LSD conviction is that there is no time except timelessness. Yet can anyone measure an activity by a trillionth of eternity? Can you measure even in light-years the length of immortality? These convictions have served to formulate and strengthen a new faith in God, a faith so satisfying and rewarding that my lasting gratitude goes to the Sandoz Pharmaceutical Laboratories which not only discovered and produced LSD-25 but are spending millions of dollars on its research. I feel they have given me a magnificent gift of a mirror in whose lovely depth one sees the reflection of all humanity.

In a sense this book has little to do either with the drug or my experiences while under its influence. As I see it, LSD merely opened a door and allowed me to look into the core of every person who lives or has lived. Many hundreds of persons given LSD have entered worlds of fantastic beauty where compassion and love have become compulsory. People who have had such experiences usually agree that deep within each of us lie goodness unimagined, wisdom, music, talents of every variety, joy, peace, humility, love, and spirituality, to mention only a few. Hidden away in each individual is a vast gold mine, but as yet only a few puny and thread-like veins have been discovered.

It is easy to scoff at such an idea, declaring quickly, "I don't believe a word of it. I haven't a speck of talent for painting, for example."

I have made similar remarks in the past. It is even extremely difficult to believe that such capacities lie within yourself after you have seen the beauty and felt the love. Denying a fact, however, has never prevented it from remaining a fact. It seems to me our fault lies, not in our lack of talent or potential, but in our refusal to believe that it exists. Only after we can accept such a belief and have thus gained enough confidence to look within ourselves can our development go full steam ahead.

Browning's poem, *Paracelsus,* tells of this need to look within:

Truth is within ourselves; it takes no rise
From outward things, whate'er you may believe.
There is an inmost center in us all,
Where truth abides in fulness; and around,
Wall upon wall, the gross flesh hems it in,
This perfect, clear perception—which is truth.
A baffling and perverting carnal mesh
Binds it, and makes all error; and to know
Rather consists in opening out a way
Whence the imprisoned splendor may escape,
Than in effecting entry for a light
Supposed to be without.

All great painting, literature, music, and religious illumination have come from within some human breast; yet I suspect that if the greatest artist or composer told himself frequently, as we often do, that he had no talent, he would soon cease to be either creative or great. Similarly every bit of warmth, love, understanding, and compassion we have ever received has come from within the person who gave it. I would not claim to know how any individual can develop his potential and liberate these qualities which lie in abundance within us. I feel sure, however, that a person must first recognize that they are there; then he might willingly work for their release, and life could become far more fulfilling than it is now.

Whenever I hear St. Paul's words, "Eye hath not seen, nor ear heard . . . the things which God hath prepared," I find myself wanting to say quite sacrilegiously, "Oh, yes, I have! And I found heaven exactly where Christ always said it would be—in the heart of every human being."

APPENDIX

by Robert S. Davidson, Ph.D.

LYSERGIC ACID DIETHYLAMIDE has remarkable clinical properties. Though most drugs are prescribed in milligrams, or thousandths of a gram, LSD-25 is measured in micrograms, or gammas, which are millionths of a gram. As little as 10 to 20 gammas may produce some physiological reactions in a human being, and 50 to 75 gammas will often produce visual images. In spite of its great potency, LSD seems to be an unusually safe drug when given in the proper dosage to carefully selected subjects.

The exact mechanism of LSD action in the brain is not yet fully known, but certain facts have been ascertained. Actually, only a small per cent of the drug reaches the brain, and this amount seems to act as a catalyst in changing the enzyme balance. Apparently because of such an imbalance, the perceptual changes continue for several hours after the LSD itself has disappeared from the brain.

Several stages of the drug's action can be distinguished. At first, there is a gradual onset of physical symptoms, beginning anywhere from fifteen minutes to two hours after the physician administers LSD by injection or orally. Typical reactions during this time are a feeling of chilliness, slight nausea, anxiety, and some clouding of consciousness, although this latter is usually slight. LSD is not like an anesthetic; the subject is always entirely conscious. The next stage, which usually starts about an hour or so after the drug is administered and continues for about six hours, is typified by marked changes in visual perception. During this time, if the subject keeps his eyes closed, he sees vivid fantasies; if he looks around him, he is likely to see the walls "breathe," colors in paintings become very vivid, the pile of a carpet acquires great depth and rich texture, or fantastic shapes appear on whatever background he is looking at. If he gazes into another person's eyes, this person's face may seem to change shape rapidly, sometimes appearing to be that of someone else the subject knows, such as a father, or sometimes contorting in quick succession into a devil, a witch, or a wild animal. It is during this period that the subject's most meaningful experiences and insights occur. He may be very quiet or tense while in this state. Many subjects feel somatic pains or pressures, often related to previous injuries and containing emotional charges which can be relieved by discussion. These pains seldom persist for long after the drug's effects have worn off. Finally the effects become less intense; if no antidote is given, perceptual distortions are virtually gone by about twelve hours after their onset. Some subjects feel sluggish and others tense for the next several days. Often they feel calm and relatively free of anxiety.

Because there are many similarities between the action of LSD and schizophrenia, the LSD experience has sometimes been referred to as the LSD psychosis. We should, however, make an important distinction here between the LSD state and actual insanity. Most persons accepted as volunteers for LSD experiments do not believe that the visions (or hallucinations) they are experiencing are any more real than a dream would be to any of us. They can separate psychic reality from external reality. Such a distinction would not be likely for a true psychotic.

Under LSD, the subject is able to have the most fantastic dreams in a waking state and report them to a companion immediately in a perfectly sensible manner. He can smoke, paint, go to the bathroom, or carry on most conventional activities which require no particular judgment. However, most subjects seem to prefer to meditate quietly. At times, a subject may feel like laughing or crying without being able to explain why he is experiencing these feelings. It is usually difficult for him to think abstractly. Though these evidences of dissociation of feeling and difficulty with abstractions are also found in psychosis, the LSD subject differs from the mentally ill person in that he nearly always knows where he is and who his attendants are. Furthermore, in the most typical psychosis, schizophrenia, the psychotic person usually has hallucinations which are auditory (hearing voices), whereas the hallucinations of the LSD subject are almost wholly visual. Under the influence of LSD, then, one is not actually insane but is in a special state of consciousness.

Although a number of experimenters have found LSD to be of value in psychotherapy, there are several general contraindications for the use of the drug. Therefore subjects who volunteer to take it need to be screened carefully. For example, persons who have had a mental illness might experience a temporary reactivation of such illness. Since any subject who has been given LSD is temporarily more likely to put his impulses into action, persons who have had suicidal tendencies need to be watched carefully if they are allowed to take the drug at all. Also LSD is not for anyone who would use it as an aid to psychological withdrawal from life's problems, a solution exemplified by the Beat-Zen addict or the marihuana user. Of course, in addition to a careful selection of the volunteers, competent research in psychotherapy requires that an experienced therapist who has had many sessions of LSD himself be in constant attendance. The physician who has given the drug has an antidote immediately available (often an injection of chlorpromazine) in case it should be needed.

The typical procedure for a psychotherapy session using LSD is to have the subject relax on a couch after the physician has administered the drug. Usually the subject wears a sleep mask to help him concentrate on the visual material which takes shape in his mind. Meanwhile, he may listen to recorded classical music. Such music is often helpful in establishing certain emotional moods and thereby aids the subject in letting his feelings come out. Frequently the subject experiences rejection, deprivation, anger, love, and sex feelings of great intensity. After these emotions are discharged, he has a wonderful feeling of relief. Whether the therapist himself be a Freudian, Jungian, Adlerian, Reichian, or Zen enthusiast, he is taxed to the limit of his knowledge by the symbolism which emerges from the human mind under LSD.

Some researchers believe that LSD shortens psychotherapy, but in the opinion of others, this point is debatable. Certainly the drug often increases the subject's awareness; his main interpersonal difficulties, however, may be almost completely bypassed. LSD is most successful with subjects whose method of coping with problems has been socially acceptable and whose interpersonal relations are, at least part of the time, sensitive and warm. On the other hand, the drug has been helpful with alcoholics and narcotic addicts in case these people are willing to accept psychotherapy.

Because tolerance to LSD builds up rapidly and because it does not consistently result in a pleasant experience, there seems to be no reason to fear addiction to the drug. If there is careful screening of subjects, no permanent psychological difficulty appears to be caused by the drug. Since distribution of LSD is carefully controlled by the manufacturer, there is no present problem for the general public. It should be stated here, however, that LSD is not likely now or in the future to be any panacea for those seeking magic happiness pills to solve their personal problems.

The hallucinogens have enjoyed a long history primarily because of their aid in relaxing the usually controlling intellect while leaving much of the ego intact. The center of one's awareness can shift and yet be comprehended and integrated into the personality. Control of the vision-producing substances has often been in the hands of the priests. Yet where the hallucinogens have been openly obtainable, as is peyote in certain of our states and in Mexico, there has been no general misuse of them, perhaps because of the uncertainty on the part of the user that his experience will be pleasant. Besides the anxiety usually felt in the early stages of a drug's action, the controlling ego is likely to try to fight off any threat to its power. The result is that frequently volunteers, instead of experiencing unity, have reported an unresolved state in which they are unable to release their emotions. As a result unusually blocked persons experience great frustration, as if a civil war were going on inside themselves. At any rate, most experimenters believe the hallucinogens themselves do not lead to drug addiction.

Readers who are interested in a lucid and comprehensive account of the state of increased awareness induced by hallucinogens may refer to Aldous Huxley's description of his mescaline experience, *The Doors of Perception.*[4] The description of the mystical experience by the psychologist William James in his book *The Varieties of Religious Experience*[5] is a classic. James has written of his personal experience in a nitrous oxide trance:

> . . . One conclusion was forced upon my mind at that time, and my impression of its truth has ever since remained unshaken. It is that our normal waking consciousness, rational

[4] Huxley, Aldous. *The Doors of Perception.* New York: Harper and Brothers, 1954.

[5] James, William. *The Varieties of Religious Experience.* New York: The Modern Library, 1929, pp. 378-9.

> consciousness as we call it, is but one special type of consciousness, whilst all about it, parted from it by the filmiest of screens, there lie potential forms of consciousness entirely different. We may go through life without suspecting their existence; but apply the requisite stimulus, and at a touch they are there in all their completeness, definite types of mentality which probably somewhere have their field of application and adaptation. No account of the universe in its totality can be final which leaves these other forms of consciousness quite disregarded. How to regard them is the question,—for they are so discontinuous with ordinary consciousness. Yet they may determine attitudes though they cannot furnish formulas, and open a region though they fail to give a map. At any rate, they forbid a premature closing of our accounts with reality. Looking back on my own experiences, they all converge towards a kind of insight to which I cannot help ascribing some metaphysical significance. The keynote of it is invariably a reconciliation. It is as if the opposites of the world, whose contradictoriness and conflict make all our difficulties and troubles, were melted into unity. Not only do they, as contrasted species, belong to one and the same genus, but *one of the species,* the nobler and better one, *is itself the genus, and so soaks up and absorbs its opposite into itself.* This is a dark saying, I know, when thus expressed in terms of common logic, but I cannot wholly escape from its authority. I feel as if it must mean something, something like what the hegelian philosophy means, if one could only lay hold of it more clearly. Those who have ears to hear, let them hear; to me the living sense of its reality only comes in the artificial mystic state of mind.

To those of us who have monitored volunteers who have taken LSD, it seems that an intelligent person who is sensitive and is relatively free, or not blocked, emotionally will generally, as did James, regard this experience as one of the most profoundly meaningful events in his life. On numerous occasions these volunteers have reported sudden insights into the essential unity of all life and the dissolution of their usual thinking in terms of opposites: good-bad, beautiful-ugly, love-hate. At times a volunteer will cry out delightedly, "How utterly simple it all is!" Since no conflict or ambivalences can exist at a moment when there is no conception of opposites, he experiences himself in complete harmony with a total absence of anxiety.

The drug does have the power to expand consciousness and to make one aware of a fundamental unity with all life processes. This increased awareness could be especially valuable to the following people: the non-neurotic, fairly well-integrated persons who are not troubled enough to seek professional psychotherapy; people who are aware of unpleasant feelings of alienation from nature and a growing dissatisfaction with our cultural goal of accumulating money and possessions; those who are discontented with mass-produced ideals and materialistic values; those who wish to be in touch with their deepest emotions instead of being constantly enmeshed in the web of abstractions spun by their own calculating intellects; and those who wish they could stop *doing* something continually so that they might have the opportunity to *be* their own individual selves.

Made in the USA
Monee, IL
13 September 2026

62973775R00128